INTO THE TRAP

INTO THE TRAP

CRAIG MOODIE

ROARING BROOK PRESS

New York

Text copyright © 2011 by Craig Moodie
Map illustration copyright © 2011 by Laszlo Kubinyi
Published by Roaring Brook Press
Roaring Brook Press is a division of Holtzbrinck
Publishing Holdings Limited Partnership
175 Fifth Avenue, New York, New York 10010
mackids.com

Library of Congress Cataloging-in-Publication Data

Moodie, Craig.
  Into the trap / Craig Moodie.—1st ed.
    p. cm.
  Summary: Twelve-year-old Eddie Atwell accidentally learns who has been
stealing lobsters from Fog Island lobstermen and enlists thirteen-year-old
Briggs Fairfield, a summer visitor, to help foil their plans.
  ISBN 978-1-59643-585-8
  [1. Robbers and outlaws—Fiction.   2. Lobster fishers—Fiction.   3. Adventure
and adventurers—Fiction.   4. Islands—Fiction.]   1. Title.

PZ7.M7723Int 2011
[Fic]—dc22

                                                          2010029238

Roaring Brook Press books are available for special promotions and premiums.
For details contact: Director of Special Markets, Holtzbrinck Publishers.

First edition 2011
Printed in May 2011 in the United States of America by
RR Donnelley & Sons Company Harrisonburg, Virginia

1 3 5 7 9 8 6 4 2

For Ellen, forever

MAINLAND

Fog Island Sound

Greenhead Island

Fog Island

the Break

Greenhead Gut

philbrick's dock

West Harbor

Tern Island

Saltworks

Atwell dock

FOG

Breakers

ATLANTIC OCEAN

N

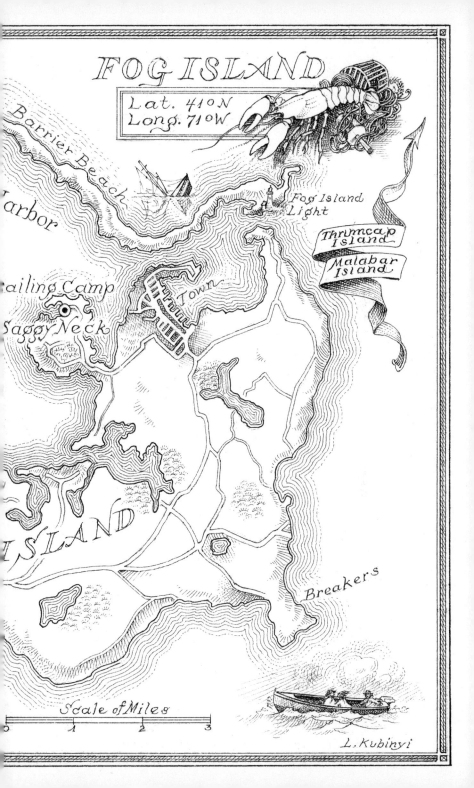

STOLEN LOBSTERS REPORTED

August 9, Fog Island Harbor—Lobsterman Walt Atwell was the latest Fog Island resident hit by the current wave of lobster thefts. On Friday, he notified police that he was missing roughly one thousand pounds of lobsters from his pound, or "car," where he keeps his catch before shipping them to mainland dealers. Chief of Police Harvey Snow said this makes the sixth theft reported since July 20, bringing the total to nearly ten thousand pounds of lobsters. "No suspects have been identified," he added.

Item in the *Fog Island Gazette*

All ships, all ships, all ships. This is the United States Coast Guard Station Fog Island. Urgent marine information broadcast. A twelve-and-a-half-foot catboat—white hull, white sail, buff trim, piloted by a thirteen-year-old male—is reported missing in the vicinity of Saggy Neck. Any mariner sighting this vessel should render assistance and contact this or any Coast Guard unit immediately on channel 16. This is Coast Guard Station Fog Island, out.

Coast Guard emergency broadcast, August 12, 9:17 a.m.

PART I

THE BAIT

CHAPTER ONE
AUGUST 12, 4:05 A.M.

EDDIE ATWELL TOOK LIGHT STEPS onto the dock, hoping to keep the warped planks from creaking, and paused by the stack of lobster traps. He looked back at the house beyond the trees. Only the dim porch light showed through the leaves. He took a deep breath and got a better grip on the fishing pole and tackle box he held in one hand and the bucket of live eels in the other. He glanced at the traps beside him stacked higher than his head. Warps coiled, buoys painted, bait bags ready, they waited to be loaded aboard *Marie A.*, his father's lobster boat, to replace the ones they'd lost to a dragger, its net clawing along the bottom in the area where they set their traps. If they'd been able to set the extra traps, they'd have all six hundred traps they were allowed in the water. But now that his dad was laid up, they were going nowhere. "The only thing worse than lost traps," his dad had said, "are dry traps. And now we've got thieves trying to put us out of business. Seems we'd do better setting traps for thieves than lobsters."

If he caught a few big striped bass, Eddie knew, he could make some money, and help his dad out.

But the only way to help was to break a promise. His mom and dad had told him they didn't want him fishing alone while they were off-island for his dad's operation.

He looked back at the house. Crickets trilled in the undergrowth. An owl made soft hoots. He shifted his weight and the planks groaned under his rubber seaboots.

But no one knew he was heading out to Greenhead Island, not even his sister Laurie.

Promise or no promise, he was going after those bass.

Beyond the traps was the floodlight his father had rigged on top of a piling. Moths swirled in the beam. He peered over to look into the submerged lobster car, a mesh pound as big as the bed of a pickup truck. In the light filtering through the water he made out the shadowy forms of only a few lobsters crawling along the bottom.

"Good luck to you, bugs," he said. "Send up a flare if anyone tries to swipe the rest of you."

He set his gear into his skiff and climbed in. He grabbed the plastic juice jug from under a seat and bailed out the water sloshing at the bottom.

The water made him shiver, and he was glad he wore jeans, his boots, and a plaid flannel shirt. He tugged his faded Red Sox cap down snug on his brown hair and yanked the starter. The outboard coughed.

"Come on," he said. "Don't give me any trouble."

He yanked again and this time the outboard spewed a cloud of smoke and sputtered to life.

He uncleated the line and shoved off. He sat down on the seat, the skiff leaning under his weight, and idled away from the dock. In the east, below the stars speckling the sky overhead, he could see the faint blue glow of dawn. The moon had already set. He steered out of the cove and throttled up as he entered the bay.

He'd never fished Greenhead Island before. It was foul with shoals and rocks, but Jake Daggett, his sister's on-and-off boyfriend, had told him striped bass might be feeding out there. "It's a secret," Jake had said. "Time I went out there, I slayed them. Big ones. Been too busy with other things to try it again. No one else bothers with it because you're more likely to hit a rock than a bass."

So what if Mom and Dad don't want me going out by myself? he thought. *How are they ever going to find out? And if I run into a school of thirty or forty pounders, and the price holds around two bucks a pound, they wouldn't mind the payday.*

Eddie hadn't been able to go lobstering since his dad hurt his shoulder. With all the shore work—painting buoys, coiling line, mending bait bags, stacking and re-pairing traps—he hadn't had a chance to go fishing at all. Not going lobstering was bad enough, but not going fishing made him feel trapped. He ached to be on the water. Even the long trip across the bay and the risk of snags or a scraped bottom would be worth getting out again. The way he had calculated it, poring over the tables in his dog-eared copy of the *Eldridge Tide and Pilot Book*, he'd be there right at the turn of the tide.

He glanced at his watch: 4:22. His parents had given him the watch, a diver's waterproof model, for his twelfth birthday back in March.

"You're always late, just like your father," his mother said. "But now you have no excuse about coming home on time." She brushed a strand of her gray-streaked brown hair off her face and smiled as he put the watch on.

His father laughed. "That's a better watch than mine," he said. "But remember: it's not a toy. It's the kind of watch a real lobsterman needs."

Eddie stood up and leaned over to hug his mother, then shook his father's hand.

"Before you know it you'll be running your own boat," his father said, "just like my dad and his dad before him."

Eddie felt heat rise into his cheeks. He looked back at the watch.

A real lobsterman. That's what he was going to be.

He pointed his bow at the horizon and opened up the throttle. The skiff unzipped the flat water of the bay. This time of day was one of his favorites, the time when daylight was only a hint on the horizon. Dawn and dusk were the best times to be alone on the water. He settled onto the stern seat and watched the water ahead of him.

He knew he didn't have to worry about Greenhead Gut, a whirlpool that could trap a small boat like his skiff. It only appeared when the tide was running hard, and now the tide was slack. He checked his watch again. His dad would be heading into the hospital in a few hours, "to see if Dr. Sawbones can fix my wing," as he had said the night before. Eddie knew that for his dad, the pain in his shoulder wasn't nearly as bad as the pain of not going lobstering—and not being able to get his lobsters back or catch the thieves himself. "You want something fixed right," his dad told him time after time, "you fix it yourself."

At first his dad hadn't even wanted to tell Chief Snow about the missing lobsters. But since he hurt his shoulder stacking traps, getting the catch back himself wasn't an option.

"Bad timing for a torn rotator cuff," he said, after he made the call to Chief Snow. "Nothing better I'd like to do than get those lobsters back—and put those poachers away. I'd poke into every cove and haul-out and creek in the marshes for any sign of them. But now we'll have to rely on the cops to do it for us. Don't hold your breath about ever seeing any of those lobsters again."

The silhouette of the island appeared in the dimness, and Eddie throttled down. Ahead the water spread out smooth, its surface salted with reflections of stars. He neared the island and idled along shore, steering past rocks sticking out of the water. When he came around the far point, he made out the shape of a small sailboat anchored in a cove.

What's that boat doing out here? he thought. *Looks like one of those boats from the sailing camp. Just what I need, some off-islander to spoil the fishing.*

He turned the skiff around and headed past a point to the other side where he'd seen the mouth of a creek.

He grabbed a burlap bag, reached into the bait bucket, and gripped an eel by the head. In the beam of light from his flashlight, it writhed and flexed and spiraled itself like a wet vine around his forearm. He held the flashlight between his teeth and reached for his hook. When he jabbed it through the eel's pale chin, then worked it up through its nose and out again, the eel jerked and unwound itself.

Then he steered around the rocks close to the mouth of the creek and cut the engine. He swung the pole outward, rose up in the skiff, and cast the eel toward a patch of grass that was almost swallowed by the high tide. The eel and weight splashed in front of the grass.

He set the drag, jigged the pole, then carefully began reeling in. As he shifted his weight, the boat rocked, sending silver pulses out across the surface. Water gathered around his boots.

He held his breath. He felt a quiver run through his hands—his own excitement. A striped bass could strike at any moment.

He gave the pole a short jerk, then kept reeling. Nothing yet.

Then he felt a jolt and a yank on the line. He was sure he had a bass on. He gripped tighter and pulled up hard to set the hook, the pole bending down in a question mark. He braced his knees against the rail of the skiff. The fish might run. He knew he couldn't manhandle it or it might throw the hook. He eased the tip of the pole upward. It stayed bowed toward the water. The pole felt heavy, the fish at the end of the line an unmoving mass.

He let out a stream of breath and shook his head.

It wasn't a bass—it was a snag. He yanked the pole sideways. He spun the tip of the pole around in circles. He laid the pole down in the skiff, got the paddle, and splashed toward the line. He gripped it and pulled, but it wouldn't budge. He picked up the pole and wound the reel as tight as it would go and pulled back, let the line go slack, then jerked the pole once more as hard as he could.

Finally he took his jackknife out of his pocket and cut the line.

Lost a lively eel, he thought. He checked his bait bucket. There were only three eels left. Maybe the water out here really was too foul for fishing. No wonder no one comes out here.

But since he made the long trip out, he wasn't going to give up yet. He tied on another leader, hook, and weight and baited the hook with another eel. Yanking on the outboard's starter rope, he got the motor going on the first pull and idled the skiff along the shore to a point of rocks. He cut the engine. He stood up in the bow and cast to a spot well off the last rock and hurried to retrieve the line.

The line went taut and he sucked in his breath, hoping the heavy tug was a fish. He pulled back to set the hook and felt the tip of the pole bending. Whatever it was wouldn't move.

That's it, he thought. Another snag.

He tried to dislodge the hook, yanking and pulling and then paddling over to the line. For the second time, he had to cut the rig free.

Two eels, two weights, two hooks, he thought. Zero bass. No percentage in it, as his dad would say.

He ran his eye along the dark form of the island close by. He'd come all this way, so he might as well see what was on it. Besides, he was hungry, and he figured blueberry bushes grew on the island. He wanted to save the peanut butter sandwich and granola bar he'd put in his tackle box for later.

He stowed his pole and yanked on the starter rope. The engine made only a small chug. He yanked again and the engine coughed, then went dead. It was quirky. Sometimes it started right up, other times it took a lot of coaxing. He didn't mind—when it ran, it flew.

The skiff and engine were Laurie's, a step up from the leaky old tub he used to take out fishing but not worth much just the same. She gave them to Eddie since she worked day and night at the ice-cream parlor in town, saving money for college, and didn't have time for the water.

Eddie gripped the handle of the starter again and gave a mighty yank. The motor wheezed.

"Evinrude, you know something?" he said to the motor. "Sometimes you're nothing but rude."

At last the outboard spat and coughed and spewed out smoke and settled into a rough whine.

He steered past a sweep of grass. Only the tips stuck above the water. No light showed from the dark hulk of the island. He pointed the flashlight at the shore.

There, between two tumbles of boulders and a shelf of rock, lay a strip of beach.

He idled through a channel between the rocks, cut the engine, and coasted to the beach. The boat landed on the sand with a wet scrape. He leaped out and hauled the boat up, then took a few steps toward the thickets.

He stopped to listen. In the woods, snowy tree crickets sang their ceaseless chime. The drowsy chirp of a lone field cricket came from somewhere in the grass. A colony of katydids yakked back and forth at each other. Water lapped at the rocks.

Without turning on his flashlight, he made his way along the tide line past a salt marsh. Why he felt as though he was trespassing, he wasn't sure. He squinted ahead and took measured steps. The sense that he was being watched came over him. He was about to turn on his flashlight when right at his feet a furious flutter erupted and burst past his face. His heart lurched and he jumped back.

"Doves," he hissed. "I flushed a couple of doves." They had been roosting on the beach because the sand retained the day's warmth.

He moved on, his heart settling. He switched on his flashlight and the beam lit a blueberry bush laden with ripe berries. As he plucked them, he popped them into his mouth one by one.

Then he worked his way back. The dawn light was turning a grainy gray, and he was beginning to make out the green of leaves and the silvery pelt of the sand.

He was almost back to his skiff when he spotted a large tidal pool right at the edge of the water by the marsh. He ran his flashlight beam over the water. Hermit crabs tiptoed away along the bank when he shined the light on them. Minnows switched this way, then that.

But there was something below them, something moving well below the surface of the water.

"What?" he said out loud.

It was a lobster claw waving through the square of a wire mesh cover.

He shined his light into the pool. In the yellow beam, he saw movement.

He blinked.

The pool was packed with lobsters.

CHAPTER TWO

AUGUST 12, 5:01 A.M.

EDDIE STARED into the tidal pool. The bottom was covered with crates, each jammed with lobsters. There was only one reason someone had gone to the trouble of putting all these lobsters way out here.

He squatted down and plunged his hand into the water to open a crate. He plucked out a two-pound lobster and hefted it in his hand. It crawled in the air, its tail snapping, and waved its banded claws to defend itself.

"Still in good shape," he said. A spunky lobster was fresh, meaning that the others in the pool hadn't been there long. He turned the lobster over the way his dad always did to check for eggs. By law, females carrying clusters of minute berrylike eggs under the tail had to be thrown back. He could tell by the two thin feelers where the tail joined the body that it was a female, but she carried no berries.

He crouched down to slip the lobster back in the water.

As he latched the crate, he heard the burble of an idling engine from across the water.

Who else would be out here? Nobody had any business on Greenhead—unless it involved these lobsters.

A searchlight flared out from where he heard the sound of the motor. He ducked and scrambled away from the pool. He squirmed on his belly beneath the blueberry bush. He eased the branches aside to peer toward the beach and his skiff.

His skiff. Will they spot it?

The boat came closer. Soon it was right up next to the pool.

"Good enough," a voice called over the sound of the engine. The engine throttled down, then fell silent. "Let's get 'em in. We're running late. Already after five. Almost light."

He heard a mosquito whine by his ear. He knew he couldn't move without crackling the branches together. His elbow poked through a rip in his shirt, grinding against the rocks and sand. He felt the mosquito land and insert its needle into his earlobe. All he could do was clench his teeth.

He heard bumps and bangs and splashing. Then someone said, "You think we have all day? Speed it up." The voice carried sharp and clear over the water.

"Like to see you try getting in this thing in the dark," came another voice.

Eddie's heart thudded. He knew that voice.

He heard a different motor, an outboard, sputter to

a start, then fall silent. Someone swore. The outboard caught again, coughed, whined up high, and finally ran evenly. He heard water spattering as the outboard sound grew closer.

Coming ashore, he thought.

Then the outboard fell silent again. He heard a deep splash, this time closer—right by the tidal pool.

Lobsters. They must be dumping crates into the pool.

"How's it look?" came the first voice.

"Packed to the doors," said the familiar voice.

"Tomorrow's the day," said the other voice. "Brown should be happy when we show up with all these. Especially after we hit Philbrick and Crossman tonight."

"I don't know why we're doing those guys. It's overkill. We've got enough."

That voice, he thought. *That voice sounds like Jake.*

"Brown doesn't think so. Okay. Let's get out of here."

The searchlight switched back on and slashed across the pool. He eased himself up to peer through the leaves and made out the silhouette of a person climbing aboard an inflatable. The beam swept past him and stopped.

"Hey, Marty, what's that?"

Marty. The other voice was Marty Powers, Jake's pal. Eddie didn't know him well, but he could picture his red, fleshy face, jut jaw, narrow eyes, smirk, and scraggly brown hair tucked behind his ears.

"Damn."

"It's a skiff."

"What's that doing out here?" said Marty. "Better get it."

Eddie froze as Jake jumped out of the inflatable onto the beach and ran to the skiff.

Jake's going to know it's mine, he thought, his heart hammering. *If I can see it from here, no way he won't recognize it. He's seen it a thousand times.*

He pressed himself closer to the ground. Sand rasped in his right ear.

Jake shoved the skiff toward the water. He stopped.

"Hey," he called. "Marty."

"What?"

"This skiff . . ." he said. "I know whose it is."

Eddie lifted his head to see Jake lean over the skiff. He heard his fishing pole rattle.

"Yeah, this is his gear. It's Eddie Atwell's. You know, Laurie's brother."

"You gotta be kidding."

"I wish," said Jake. "Look at this. There's still eels in the bucket. Kid came out here bassing, just like I told him. Can you believe it?"

"You told him to come out here? Are you an idiot?"

"I told him I fished in this spot once. Before all this started. What do you think, I'm stupid enough to tell him to come out here to see what's going on?"

"This is not good," said Marty. "If Brown finds out . . ."

"Hey, Brown's your buddy."

"He's not my buddy. He's just a dealer dude I know."

"What do we do with the skiff?"

Marty exhaled. "If Brown finds out . . ."

"You already said that. Maybe he didn't see them."

"But if he did . . . we better take his skiff. Buy us some time."

"We can't just leave him out here."

Eddie saw Jake look around.

"Hey, Eddie?" he called. "Where are you?"

Eddie held his breath.

"Will you shut up?" said Marty.

Eddie felt his heart clench.

"Kid's going to rat us out," said Marty.

"Doubt that," said Jake. "I know his dad, and no son of his is going to the cops, even if it's about his lobsters. He'd tell his dad first, and his dad's off-island. We've got time. Don't you know that what happens on the water stays on the water?"

"When it comes to his catch?" said Marty. "I'm not buying it. That's his livelihood, and the kid knows it. And what happens afterward, when he does tell his dad? Did you think about that? We better tell Brown and get the lobsters over to him right away. Or find the kid. Man, I can't believe this. I've got no time left. I've got to get over to camp. But if we take the skiff, he can't go anywhere. We'll come back out later to . . ." He said something else but he must have turned his back because Eddie couldn't make out what it was.

Whatever Marty had said, he knew it wasn't good.

"And don't you go saying anything to Laurie about the kid," he heard Marty say. "You know we need her to . . ."

Jake splashed into the water, drowning out the last words.

Eddie strained his ears. What had Jake said about Laurie?

Eddie saw Jake's figure wading into the water. Jake tied the skiff to the back of the inflatable, and a few moments later the inflatable's outboard whined to life.

A charge of electricity sizzled through him. He had to get off the island. They would be back for him. And they were taking his skiff. He couldn't swim all the way back to shore. He'd be stuck on the island for who knew how long. And between him and land lay Greenhead Gut. He'd never be able to swim through it.

He heard the bigger boat's engine start up. He lifted his head and inched forward to look out from beneath the bush. He squinted and made out a name on the transom: *Nuthin's Easy*.

It was Jake's leaky old lobster boat.

Jake tied the inflatable to the stern and climbed aboard. Eddie's skiff floated behind the inflatable.

Eddie pictured himself making a break for the skiff. He could throw himself into it and stay out of sight till they towed the skiff away from the island. Then he could slip the line and drift away.

There was just one problem. He couldn't make himself move. He was paralyzed as he watched the boat idle away, towing his skiff behind it. He might as well have been a boulder on the beach.

He heard *Nuthin's Easy* throttle up.

Too late, he thought. *Too late to try to get aboard.*

He lay beneath the bush, watching the boat recede from view. The branches picked and scratched at him every time he breathed. As he listened to the sound of the engine diminish, his thoughts kept returning to Laurie. Could she really be wrapped up in this? Marty said that they needed her . . . for what? He tried to picture her agreeing to help them but the thought made him lightheaded. It couldn't be true.

But what if it were true?

Thinking about Laurie wouldn't get him off the island. He checked his watch: 5:25, about twenty minutes before sunrise. Every moment that passed was a moment closer to Marty and Jake coming back to look for him. He didn't want to think what would happen if they found him. They wouldn't kill him, would they? Jake? He couldn't take that chance. He'd have to find a place to hide.

He strained his eyes to see between the branches. The crickets continued their low hiss. A gull whined. The sound of *Nuthin's Easy* was only a low buzz in the distance.

If only he hadn't come ashore, he thought, he'd still have a boat.

Wait a minute, he thought. *The other boat.* What about the boat he'd seen earlier, that small sailboat anchored in a cove around the far point when he first came out to the island?

He pushed his way out of the blueberry bush, brushed himself off, and took off down the beach, his boots clumping in the sand.

CHAPTER THREE

AUGUST 12, 5:40 A.M.

HE JOGGED along the water's edge, hoping to spot the boat, till he reached a boulder jutting from the beach. It was sloped enough for him to scale it. He clambered up, careful not to scrape his hands on the barnacles, and stood at the top, catching his breath. He scanned the cove and the water lying between Greenhead Island and the band of dunes on the outer beach. Everywhere he looked, the water was empty.

Too late, he thought. *But maybe the boat was around the next point.*

He jumped off the rock and sprinted down the beach, skirted boulders and clattered over rocks, cut up over a ledge into the woods, and pushed his way through the underbrush to a bluff overlooking the beach, a sand spit, and the water beyond.

There, out on the water, sat the boat, its sail slack.

Eddie took a deep breath, cupped his hands around

his mouth, and yelled, "Hey, you in the sailboat! Over here!"

The first rays of the sun were sparkling across the water. Eddie saw the sailor sit up and look around.

"Over here!" he yelled again, waving his arms.

This time the sailor started to stand up but he hit his head on the boom and sat back down hard. Then he looked at Eddie, waving at him with one hand and rubbing his head with the other.

"Can you give me a ride?" Eddie yelled. He saw the sailor wave again and begin working the tiller. The rudder swished the water as the sailor moved it back and forth like a single oar or scull. But the boat swung away from Eddie.

"I'll be right down," yelled Eddie. The bluff was too steep for him to slide down, so he backtracked through the undergrowth. He broke onto the beach and ran along the water toward the boat.

The boat had drifted farther off.

"Hey," he called, this time not as loud, knowing how well sound carried over water. "You coming to get me?"

"Sorry," called the sailor. Eddie could see that he was a lanky kid with glasses and a mop of blond hair. The kid peered at the sail, then back at Eddie.

"The current is taking me away from shore. And there's another problem."

"What's that?" said Eddie. A greenhead fly landed on his forehead. He slapped at it.

24

The kid looked up at the limp sail, then back at Eddie.

"I really haven't got the hang of it . . . I'm hopeless."

Eddie cocked his head.

"What?" he said.

"It's what my sailing instructor told me, though in a pleasant sort of way. I really don't know how to sail."

Eddie frowned. *Here I am*, he thought, *trapped on Greenhead Island with two thieves about to come after me, and I've got a rich kid from the sailing school that can't sail bobbing fifty yards away.* What was he doing out here, anyway, if he couldn't sail?

"Don't do anything," said Eddie. "I'll swim out to you."

Eddie shucked off his boots and waded into the water. It was cold as it closed over his jeans. When he was up to his waist, he held his boots above the surface and sidestroked his way to the boat.

"I suggest you climb in from the stern," said the kid, peering over the rail at him. "You can get a good purchase on the rudder with your foot."

"Purchase?" said Eddie, spitting seawater.

"A good hold—grip."

"Right. I'm coming up. Watch out for my boots."

Eddie heaved the boots over the rail. One sailed high and the kid raised an arm to fend it off but it knocked his glasses askew before it bounced into the cockpit with the other boot.

"Sorry," said Eddie.

"No need to apologize," said the kid, inspecting his glasses. "Entirely my fault."

Eddie got a toehold on the rudder gudgeon, the fitting where the rudder joined the transom. Then he grabbed the top and hoisted himself up. He belly-flopped over the rail and tumbled with a splash into the cockpit.

"Welcome aboard," said the kid, sitting on the deck with both hands on the tiller. His skinny legs stuck out of khaki shorts and ended in floppy white socks and leather boat shoes. He wore a navy blue short-sleeve shirt with an alligator emblem. His collar was flipped up.

He extended a gangly arm and offered his hand.

"Briggs Fairfield," he said, "Bedford Hills, New York."

Eddie eased his hand upward and wiped it on his sopping clothes. The shirt was as wet as his hand. Water puddled around him on the wooden deck. He touched his drenched cap, then rubbed his palm on his pants leg.

"Ah, hi," he said, taking Briggs's hand. "Eddie Atwell. Sorry about, you know, the boot."

Eddie tried to let go of his hand but Briggs held on for a moment. Then Eddie gripped again as Briggs let go. Finally they dropped each other's hand.

He noticed that a strip of frayed adhesive tape was wrapped around the right temple of Briggs's tortoise-shell glasses and that he had a lanyard attached to them so if they got knocked off, he wouldn't lose them.

Geek.

Briggs tilted his head.

"Not at all," he said. "You hardly had a choice in the matter."

Eddie paused. Should he tell this total stranger anything about what happened? He knew that Marty worked as a counselor at the sailing camp. Maybe it would be better if Briggs didn't know.

"Listen," he said, unbuttoning his flannel shirt. "I'm in kind of a jam. It's long story. But you think we can head for the cove where I live? I need to get back as fast as I can. It's in that direction."

Briggs shrugged. "I'm afraid we're not going anywhere," he said. "When I came out here last night, the breeze was blowing beautifully."

"Once the sun gets higher," said Eddie, "the breeze will come with it. And we can always paddle, right?"

He pulled off his sopping flannel shirt and T-shirt. He wrung them out and pulled them on again. "But we won't have to paddle," he said. "See? Over there, there's a patch of ripples. Means a breeze is already heading our way."

Briggs sat up and poked his glasses tight to the bridge of his nose. He squinted in the direction Eddie pointed.

"Ah, yes," he said, blinking. "You have sharp eyes." He looked back at Eddie. "I hope you don't mind me asking," he said, "but are you in danger?"

Eddie felt the breeze wash over him. The sail stirred, waved, filled. He didn't want to tell Briggs anything. Maybe if he simply clammed up, the question would pass.

"Better steer that way," he said, pointing toward the distant shore.

Briggs pulled the tiller toward him, and the boat slipped ahead. The rigging creaked and the boat felt as though it was lifting. A puff filled the sail and the boat heeled for a moment, leaning over as the sail grew heavy with the wind. The rail dipped and water gurgled past. Eddie glanced at Briggs and saw that he was biting his lip. He gripped the tiller so hard his knuckles bulged. He pushed the tiller away from him to bring the bow to point into the wind. The sail fluttered and the boat leveled and slowed.

"Why'd you do that?" said Eddie.

"I'm not a big fan," said Briggs, licking his lips and looking up at the sail, "of heeling over too far."

"We'll never get anywhere this way."

Briggs nodded.

"I realize that, which is why I'm bringing us back on course now."

He eased the tiller back and the wake began making a chuckling sound. The boat gained momentum, settling back as the puff subsided, and eased across the smooth water.

Was he nervous about sailing? A kid from a sailing camp?

Briggs glanced at Eddie. "Don't mind me," he said. "I just get a little jumpy when the boat starts going fast."

Eddie shrugged.

"Don't worry about it," he said. "I've never sailed a boat before, only handled skiffs and fishing boats with engines, but wouldn't you want to pull in that rope there? The wind is almost on our nose, so the sail should be in tighter."

"You mean the sheet," said Briggs, pulling in the line. "You're right. That's much better." He cleared his throat as the boat gained speed. "See what I mean about being hopeless? I've been trying to learn to sail since July. Actually my parents have been trying to teach me to sail for years. Dinghy lessons. Charters. But still I haven't got the basics down, the efforts of my sailing instructor notwithstanding. But this isn't so bad."

Eddie eyed Briggs. "So, what are you doing out here if you can't sail?"

Briggs pushed his glasses up. "I'll make a deal with you," he said. "If you tell me why you're out here, then I'll tell you why I am."

Eddie lifted his cap and ran his hand through his hair. He figured he didn't need to know why Briggs had sailed to Greenhead Island. But he did need his help getting back.

"Okay," he said, leaning against the rail. "It started when Jake Daggett, my sister's boyfriend, told me about his secret fishing spot on Greenhead. But it turns out Jake wasn't going there for the fishing at all."

CHAPTER FOUR

"**So I found them,**" said Eddie. "All those lobsters."

The breeze was picking up as the sun climbed, and the boat heeled through the bright wavelets. Eddie glanced at Briggs, who kept steering too far into the wind, so they'd lose headway and have to fall off the wind to let the sail fill again.

Briggs made sailing look hard, thought Eddie. But how hard could it be? Maybe he should offer to take over. He could see that Briggs kept licking his dry lips. But if he offered, he might make Briggs more nervous.

Briggs looked at him. "Are a lot of the lobsters out there your father's? How will he get them back?"

Eddie looked up and squinted against the sun.

"That's what I'm trying to figure out."

Briggs peered up at the sail and worked the tiller. "But what if the thieves come back for them? Why wouldn't you tell the police? Time would seem to be of the essence."

He patted the front pocket of his shorts. "I've got my cell phone. Why not put in a call to the police, if we have any service out here?"

Eddie shook his head. "No way. My dad called Chief Snow about the thefts, but he didn't want to. He's never really gotten along too well with him. Says Chief Snow thinks of lobstermen as crooks with traps. So he wanted to track down the thieves himself."

"Not much faith," said Briggs, "in the authorities?"

"The police?"

"Yes."

"He's a waterman," said Eddie. "He takes care of his own business."

He looked out at the water.

There was another reason he couldn't tell the police. That would be selling out Laurie—if she were involved.

"What do you think they'll do to you," said Briggs, his voice quiet, "if they—how should I put this—if they track you down?" He glanced at Eddie, then looked away.

Eddie shrugged. "What do you mean?"

Briggs looked back at him.

"Do you think," he said, his voice even quieter, "that they'd try to hurt you? That they might . . . try to silence you?"

"Silence me?" said Eddie. He laughed, but it sounded more nervous than he liked. "I just don't know."

Eddie got up and climbed to the bow. He gripped the forestay and leaned against the mast, riding up and down with the boat.

Would Jake or Marty really do it, he thought. *Would they really try to hurt me? Or that guy Brown? Would he?* He squeezed his eyes shut.

If he told the police, he might get Laurie in trouble. His dad couldn't help, at least not right now. But he could try to get the lobsters back himself. By then, his dad would be home from the mainland. They could divvy up the catch with the other lobstermen and sell them before Jake and Marty even knew the lobsters were missing.

He opened his eyes and scanned the water again. It was a risk—like a lobster knowing that it was heading into the trap just to get the bait. He could get in, but could he get out? His only choice was to do what his dad would have done: get the lobsters back himself.

But how would he do that without his skiff?

He turned to Briggs.

"How about you?" he said. "Why were you out there?"

"It's hardly as dramatic as your story," said Briggs. "I was simply attempting to escape from camp and a certain counselor who had become my nemesis."

Eddie frowned.

"Your what?"

"My archenemy. He hated me from the moment I set foot in camp."

Briggs let go of the tiller to clean his glasses. With his glasses off, he blinked and squinted as if he were trying to see in the dark. The sail began to flap, and he grabbed the tiller again.

"He never made any pretense about hating me," he said, flipping the lanyard over his head and slipping the glasses back on. "Maybe it was because he thought I was mocking him."

"Mocking him how?"

"Promise not to laugh?"

Eddie almost laughed right that moment, but he didn't.

"Promise."

"Sometimes, I seem to mimic people's intonations and accents," he said. "I'm not sure why I do it. Maybe I get nervous. But I've done it when I'm not nervous, too. I don't try to do it. It just happens. One time my parents and I went to a dude ranch in Wyoming and I picked up the phrase 'boy howdy.' To this day I don't know what 'boy howdy' means, but I began using it out there. People looked at me like I was cracked. A flatlander kid trying to sound like a cowpoke. I never learned to stay in the saddle, either."

"So did you say 'boy howdy' to this counselor?"

He shook his head.

"No, I said 'pizza.' Only the way he pronounced it was

'peets-er.' He doesn't pronounce an *R* except where it doesn't belong. I was nervous around him from the time he tripped me on the first morning. One day he said that we were having pizza for dinner, and I said that I adored peets-er, mimicking him without meaning to. I could tell by the way he narrowed his evil slit eyes that he thought I was making fun of him. That seemed to trigger it, that and my Yankees cap."

"Well," said Eddie, "the cap alone would be enough to make any Red Sox fan hate you." He jumped back into the cockpit and sat down.

Briggs looked at him.

"Kidding," said Eddie.

"But don't get mad at me," said Briggs, "if I start pronouncing Sox—*Sauwcks*—the way you do. It's beyond my control."

"What, do I make you nervous?" said Eddie. He looked at the sail and sat up. It was beginning to flap.

"No, no. But this counselor detested me from the first time he smelled me."

"Smelled you?" said Eddie.

"That very first day, when I bumped into him as I first mounted the sagging stairs to the cabin, he said, 'You smell.' I asked him of what. 'Of money,' he said. 'And it stinks.' After that, he started waking me up in the middle of the night for no reason. Kicking me in the shins when we played soccer. Shoving me when I wasn't looking. Giving me latrine duty all the time. But I decided that I had to endure it. My parents are on a trip to Spitsbergen, so it's almost impossible to have them come get me. I'm not sure they'd allow me to leave, in any case, since I was forced to attend this prison of a camp to uphold the family tradition of learning the art of sailing."

"Spitsbergen?" said Eddie.

"An archipelago above the Arctic Circle, north of Norway."

"Oh, yeah," said Eddie. He glanced at the sail. It was slack and fluttering.

"But there was one last straw that made me decide to leave," Briggs continued.

"Uh, Briggs?" Eddie said, fighting an urge to grab the tiller.

"Hmm?"

"Check the sail."

"Oh, right. Sorry."

Briggs pulled the tiller toward him to bring the bow through the wind. The sail filled again, and the boat regained momentum.

Eddie looked out at the water. If only this boat could go faster.

"There was one thing I looked forward to at camp besides going home, and that was sailing when Sallie Hodge was my instructor. She was nice to me, too. One afternoon when we were putting the gear back in the boathouse, the archfiend saw us chatting. It turned out he and Sallie had dated at one point, and he remained perversely jealous of her. His jealousy was ridiculous, of course. Sallie treated me like a kid brother.

"That was the same day as the talent show, in which I was going to play guitar. My talents are few, but I do know my way around a twelve-string acoustic. On my way to the auditorium for my performance that evening, he came up behind me, carrying sailing gear. Suffice it to say that things ended up in a bad place for me because he was infuriated that Sallie had given me attention. I decided to leave the camp that night."

Eddie was watching the water ahead. He did not like what he saw.

"You see that?" said Eddie, standing up again and stepping onto the foredeck. "It's right where we have to go. The Gut's already looking bad. Listen. It sounds like rapids. Hear it?"

"My only escape was by water," said Briggs. Eddie turned to look at him. How could he still be talking when they were about to face the Gut?

"That very night," Briggs went on, now letting the sail luff and the boat lose headway, "last night, I took one of the Beetle Cats, the only sailboat I feel at all comfortable handling, thanks to Sallie. It was around two, and I had stuffed a bunch of my clothes under my covers to make them think I was still in my cot. I wanted to sail to the mainland. But the breeze quit, and I found myself by the island where I found you. Do you want to know what the worst part was?"

"Briggs," said Eddie, standing at the bow, gripping the forestay with both hands. "I need you to pay attention."

Less than a quarter mile away, a standing wave was rearing up, a breaking crest sliding down its face. Briggs's face went blank and his mouth dropped open.

Chapter Five

BRIGGS HAD CLOSED HIS MOUTH and was gripping on to the tiller so hard his fists quivered. He was making a high-pitched whistling sound, though his lips weren't moving.

"Briggs, get a hold of yourself!" said Eddie. "Is that you making that sound?"

Briggs was whistling like the wind whining in a partly open window.

He stopped and looked at Eddie.

"What? Sorry," he said. "I whistle when I'm scared."

"Don't be scared," said Eddie. "Just be ready. We'll need all the speed we can get to make it through the Gut."

"Maybe you should take the tiller," said Briggs. "I don't know if I can do it."

"You can do it, Briggs. You know more about sailing than I do."

"I don't know. I don't know if I can handle it in water like that."

Eddie glanced at Briggs.

"You know more about sailing than you think you do," he said.

Briggs said nothing. His gaze was fixed, his face pale. The whistle began again.

Ahead the water appeared to bulge and tilt, as if an inflating balloon was spreading across the surface of the bay.

"We're almost in it," said Eddie. "Briggs?"

Briggs still hadn't blinked.

Eddie grabbed the tiller as the boat rushed up the face of the first wall of water.

"Got it," he said.

"They . . . they told us about the Gut at camp," said Briggs. "No one was allowed to come out here. I never thought that I'd have to go . . ."

"Whoa. Look at that," said Eddie, his heart whirring with excitement. "Hold on, Briggs."

The boat plowed into an area of churning water that spread out as far as Eddie could see. From the break in the dunes beyond the marsh, rollers from the open ocean swept in. The crash and hiss of rapids filled Eddie's ears, drowning out Briggs's whistling. Swirls spun around the boat, boiling up froth and small waves that broke into each other.

The boat whirled around. For a moment Eddie felt dizzy.

"Look," said Eddie, raising his hands. "The tiller's flapping free. I can't steer—current's controlling it."

The tiller switched back and forth as the waves and swirls shoved the rudder.

The boat spun around so they faced the waves they'd just passed through.

"Watch your head!" said Briggs.

The sail made a crack as it got back winded and the boom swung hard to port.

"Are we going anywhere?" said Briggs. "Are we out of control?"

"We're going in circles," said Eddie.

Briggs held his head low, then slid a look at him.

"Good thing you seem to be a natural," he said. "If you hadn't taken the tiller, we would have been . . . look out!"

A roller crashed over them, heeling the boat over hard. Eddie and Briggs tumbled to the deck. The boat shot forward, then lurched upward on a wave and bounded down the other side. Eddie pulled himself up and grabbed the tiller. He felt the rush of water wrench the rudder to one side. He pulled hard and kept the boat on a straight heading.

"Got control again," said Eddie.

He pulled the tiller toward him and the bow swung through the wind, sending the boom around. Another swirl shoved the stern but Eddie brought the boat back on course.

"It's flattening out ahead," said Briggs.

"That's better," said Eddie, steering into the smoother water. The boat stabilized and gained speed as the riot of waves dropped astern. He checked behind them, then looked forward.

"I think we're good now," he said. "Water's clear ahead."

He scanned the horizon. He reminded himself to keep his eyes open for *Nuthin's Easy*. It could appear out of nowhere. But all he saw were sails toward Seal Point.

"No sign of Jake and Marty," he said, "at least for now. But see those sailboats over there? Are they from the camp?"

"That's right," said Briggs, looking across the water. Then he swiveled his head, his eyes narrowing, to look back at Eddie. "Wait one minute. What was that you said?"

"That I saw some sailboats."

"No, before that."

"You mean about Jake and Marty?"

Briggs's eyes grew large.

"Marty. Marty Powers is the name of my nemesis. Powers of Evil to me—not that I call him that to his face, of course."

"Marty Powers," he said, looking at Briggs. "That's the guy."

Briggs clutched the wooden lip of the cockpit coaming and closed his eyes. He let out a long stream of breath.

"My worst nightmare come true," he whispered. "If

Marty finds you, he finds me. I've blundered right into the trap. The trap he set for me. My nemesis will snatch me up like a lobster and plunge me into a pot of boiling water."

"Marty didn't set any trap. He doesn't know you're with me."

Briggs shot Eddie a look.

"You do not know Marty the way I know Marty."

Eddie saw Briggs's eyes shift and his mouth drop open.

"Hold on!" Eddie shouted. "Watch that wave!"

Another breaker poured past them, spinning them around, but the wind gusted and helped drive them toward calm water. Soon the whirlpools and suds were a distant hiss.

"I have to say," he said, "if it weren't for my abject fear and the news about Marty, that would have been one of the most exhilarating experiences I've ever had. Though I'm not sure I'd like to repeat it."

Eddie was watching the far shore where the sails appeared like tiny shark's teeth.

"Everyone's getting out on the water for the morning," Briggs said. "At least I have a reprieve from that torture."

Eddie shielded his eyes as he looked toward the sails.

"When do you think they're going to realize you're missing?"

Briggs scratched his cheek.

"Soon, probably. They'll make a big production of it, to make themselves look good."

"Can't imagine that they want a missing kid on their hands," said Eddie.

"All the more reason I have to get to the mainland," said Briggs, brushing his hair off his forehead. "And to think that I had chickened out. I was going back to face another three weeks at camp because I was afraid to sail on. Now, I simply must make it to the mainland. Whether I'm terrified of the prospect or not."

Eddie looked around the boat.

"In this? It's a long way." He shook his head. "I'd say you were smart to turn back."

"But I lost my nerve," said Briggs. "Just like I lost it in the Gut. And to be honest I'm not sure I have the nerve to sail solo to the mainland. In this, as you say."

"Well, you had the nerve to take off in the first place. Why didn't you just tell someone about Marty?"

"I told Mr. Kendrick, the head of the camp, but he said that it was impossible for me to leave because my parents were out of the country."

"There's another way," said Eddie. "If I got my skiff back, I could take you off-island."

He saw Briggs tilt his head.

"You'd do that?" he said, slipping his glasses off. "You'd take me to the mainland?"

"You're helping me. Least I can do is help you."

"I appreciate that, Eddie," said Briggs. He replaced his

glasses and looked up at the sail. "You know, the only way to find your skiff is to start with where you saw it last."

"Last I saw it, it was heading away from me fast, tied to the stern of *Nuthin's Easy*."

"So maybe where *Nuthin's Easy* is," said Briggs, "your skiff is, too. Or might be."

Eddie looked across the water.

"If I had my skiff back, I could go out to Greenhead Island and get my dad's lobsters back."

Briggs raised his eyebrows. "What if you ran into Jake and Marty?"

"Can't worry about that right now. Got to get the skiff back first. Then we can go after the lobsters."

"*We?*" said Briggs, raising his eyebrows.

"Yeah. After we get the lobsters, we take you to the mainland."

"I don't know," said Briggs. "The question is am I desperate enough to possibly face Marty again?"

"You think you're desperate?" said Eddie, the words coming out faster than he expected. "My dad can't make a living. Everything he worked for is gone. He's in the hospital. What my dad's been working for is what I'm working for, too."

He paused. He felt his pulse speeding. He took a breath to calm himself.

"If I go to the police, we might lose the lobsters anyway," he said, trying to measure his words. "How will they keep them fresh? How will they divide them up? If we get them ourselves, they'll be safe. Dad knows all the lobstermen who were hit, and they know how much they lost. When he gets back he can get everyone together and divvy them up. The only way to do it right is to do it yourself. And anyway, you won't have to go back to camp to face your . . . your nemesis, either, because once we're done, I'll take you to the mainland the way I said I would."

Eddie took another deep breath. He saw Briggs nibble on his lower lip. Briggs took his glasses off and rubbed the bridge of his nose. He cleared his throat. He cleaned his glasses on his shirttail.

Then he replaced his glasses and shook his head. He looked at Eddie.

"Okay," he said. "I promise to help you get those lobsters back if you promise to help me get off the island."

"I told you I would."

"I will not return to prison camp. My stomach seethes at the thought. I would rather . . ."

"Chill, would you?"

"I simply do not have it in me to face my nemesis another time."

Eddie looked at Briggs.

"You won't have to," he said. He offered his hand. "Ready?"

Briggs looked at it, then at Eddie.

"As ready as I'll ever be," he said.

This time their hands locked together with ease.

Eddie pictured returning with a load of lobsters and filling up the lobster car. A spark of excitement tingled along his spine and out his fingers.

If he could do it before his father returned—bring all the stolen lobsters back where they belonged—he could be the one to keep their business alive.

That's what Dad would do. That's what a real lobsterman would do.

His dad would be proud of him—so proud.

Eddie pointed across the water. "See that small island out that way?" he said. "That's Tern Island. Our place is just around the other side, on West Fog. Jake keeps his boat over in Saltworks Cove, out by Tom Barlow's Head, not that much beyond our place. We could sail over there to see if he put his boat on his mooring. And if my skiff's with it."

"I vow never to return to Saggy Neck Sailing Camp—and Marty's clutches," said Briggs.

"Well, we've got a long way to go before we can get you off-island," said Eddie. "So we better get moving. And Briggs?"

Briggs peered at him.

"What is it?"

"No more whistling, okay?"

CHAPTER SIX
AUGUST 12, 8:39 A.M.

THE BREEZE DROPPED when they rounded the point by Saltworks Cove. The small inlet lay ahead, with a salt marsh surrounding it. Eddie sniffed the rich scent of fish, salt, and mud coming from the marsh.

"I better get down," he said, "in case Jake's on his boat. Marty's probably not there. I heard him say he had to go to work."

"His work of tormenting me," said Briggs. "Think how disappointed he'll be when he finds out I'm missing."

Eddie slid his legs beneath the foredeck and kept his head just above the raised wooden lip of the cockpit coaming to peer ahead.

On shore a broken fish shanty leaned at a crooked angle in the tall reeds and grasses of the marsh, its one window smashed, its shingles warped and cracked. A great black-backed gull perched on its bowed roof peak. A rickety wooden walkway led across the marsh to a dock with missing planks like pulled teeth. In the deeper water of the cove, *Nuthin's Easy* rode on her mooring, the inflatable tied off her stern.

"Skiff's not there," whispered Eddie. "Do you see anyone on board?"

"Everything looks deserted," said Briggs. "How close do you want me to sail?" He eased the tiller back and forth as the boat headed toward *Nuthin's Easy*.

"We better not hang around here too long," said Eddie. "Jake might be on board or coming back."

"You might not want to give up so quickly," said Briggs. "You've got to think like a thief to foil a thief."

Eddie looked back at him. "Watch where you're going," he said. "We're heading dead for the inflatable."

"What I'm suggesting," Briggs went on, "is that Jake can't afford to have anyone spot your skiff. Not yet. Later on, after he and Marty know how they will silence you . . ."

Eddie shot him a look.

"Don't be so quick to kill me off, will you?"

"I'm only hypothesizing," said Briggs. "Uh-oh."

He shoved the tiller away from him but the bow veered directly into the back of the inflatable. The boat lurched and the boom swung around with a clatter of rigging.

"Briggs, for crying out loud," said Eddie, sliding all the way underneath the foredeck. "Watch where you're going."

Briggs stood up and pushed the boat off the inflatable.

He ducked as the boom swung back around and the boat sliced off across the cove.

"Hey! What the hell are you doing?"

A figure stepped into the pilothouse door of the *Nuthin's Easy*.

"*That's Jake!*" hissed Eddie.

"Better watch it, kid," said Jake from the boat. "What are you sailing way over here for, anyway? Isn't that one of those toy boats from the sailing camp?"

"Sorry!" called Briggs as the boat moved away. "I miscalculated my course, which happens on occasion when I'm tacking in close quarters. I offer you my sincere apologies."

Eddie heard Jake laugh.

"Whatever, kid," called Jake. "You better get yourself out of here. This cove is off limits to off-islanders."

"What's he doing?" whispered Eddie.

"I can assure you that I will," called Briggs to Jake. Then, out of the corner of his mouth, he said, "He's getting into the inflatable. And he's threatening me."

"Keep heading in this direction," said Eddie. "Put some distance between us. Make it look like you're heading out of the cove. I'll tell you one thing. He didn't sound as though he knew anything about a kid missing from camp. But when he finds out, he'll put two and two together for sure."

Eddie heard the outboard on the inflatable rev to life.

"Where's he going?" he said to Briggs.

"Looks like he's going to the dock. We'll just keep on this heading. He'll think he scared me off. But I have to tell you that I didn't like his tone."

"He didn't sound that mad."

Briggs shook his head. "He was—momentarily, anyway. That's the most dangerous kind, Eddie. The kind that lulls you into believing that he's as phlegmatic as the next guy but then he explodes the next moment."

"*Phleg* what?"

"*Phlegmatic*. Easy-going. Nonchalant."

"I don't know, Briggs. I think you're overreacting. I've never seen Jake explode at anything. You must be thinking of someone else."

Briggs shrugged and looked over his shoulder. "Maybe you're right. Maybe I'm confusing Jake with Marty."

"Where's Jake now? Can you still see him?"

"He's pulling up to the dock. Now what I was suggesting before is that Jake wouldn't want anyone to see your skiff. He hasn't decided how he's going to keep you quiet. So until he lays his dastardly plan, what would he do with it?"

Eddie snorted. "Dastardly plan? Briggs, you're something else. How old are you, anyway?"

Briggs peered at him through his glasses.

"Thirteen going on fourteen."

"You talk like you're a professor or something."

Briggs laughed. "That's what my father says: 'You're

an old soul, Briggsy.' I've always spent a great deal of time with adults and books."

He gazed across the water toward the marsh.

"Eddie, think about where Jake might have hidden your skiff. Look around at all the cattails and phragmites in the marsh. They're almost as tall as our mast. He could have easily hidden your skiff among them."

"Where's Jake now?" said Eddie.

"Walking up the dock."

Eddie slid out from beneath the foredeck and peered over the rail. He saw Jake approach the shanty. The gull jeered and lifted its wings and floated off the roof. Jake passed along the front of the shanty, his shadow rippling along the shingles, opened the door, and disappeared inside.

"Okay," said Eddie. "He can't see us now. And you know something? You might be right."

He remembered what his father had said about looking up every creek in the marsh for the stolen lobsters. Why not do the same for a stolen skiff?

"There's a creek running through the marsh on the other side of the shanty," he said. "Let's go over there and take a look."

"Even with Jake there?" said Briggs, glancing ashore.

"Not much choice if we're going to take a look."

"Very well, then," said Briggs, turning to nod at Eddie. "Ready about."

"Ready about what?"

"It's a sailing term. It means that we're getting ready to come about. At least I've been able to learn some of the nautical terms, if not actually put them into practice."

"Okay," said Eddie. "Ready about."

"Hard alee!"

"Not so loud," said Eddie.

"Sorry," whispered Briggs.

Eddie shook his head as Briggs pushed the tiller away from him and the bow swung through the wind. The boom crossed over and the sail filled. Briggs adjusted the sheet and the boat jumped ahead on its new course.

"I think you're getting the hang of it, Briggs," said Eddie. "Maybe talking a little less would help your sailing a lot."

Briggs closed his eyes.

"Talking less," he said, "is something I seem to be incapable of doing."

"See that opening in the marsh?" said Eddie. "Head for it. That's the mouth of the creek."

"Awfully close to the shanty. Let's hope your friend Jake doesn't decide to reappear."

Briggs steered the boat into the creek and tightened the sheet. The sail slapped and then went slack as soon as they entered, the walls of reeds beside them screening off the breeze.

Eddie pulled the paddle out from underneath the foredeck.

"Keep your eyes open," he said, leaning over to take a stroke with the paddle, "and your voice down. No telling what we'll find down here. Looks like a trap to me."

As they came around a bend, five black ducks broke from the water, flapping and quacking as they cleared the tops of the reeds. They veered overhead, their wings whistling as they passed.

"Jeeze!" gasped Briggs.

Eddie stabbed the water with the paddle, casting a quick look over his shoulder.

"Just ducks," said Eddie. "I don't know about this. The creek goes a long way in."

A greenhead fly landed on the back of his neck and drilled into his flesh, sending a hot shiver coursing through him.

"Ow!" he yelled, slapping at the fly. The welt felt like a button of fire. "Watch out for the greenheads," he said. "They know we're here."

He paddled harder, bringing the boat around a small point deeper into the reeds. The channel took another turn. He paddled on, but the channel narrowed till the reeds closed in on either side of the boat. The boat's rails brushed against the stalks.

He felt a fly tap against his neck but before he could smack it, it had bitten him hard. He slapped at it and it circled back for seconds. He slapped again and crushed its plump body against his cheek. He felt welts from the bites rising on his skin.

"Bloodthirsty devils," said Briggs.

Fat flies swirled above Eddie's head. He tried to keep his head low as they swooped down. He gritted his teeth.

"I hate to say this," said Briggs, waving at a fly, "but it looks like this might be a dead end. Do you want me to paddle for a while?"

"No, thanks," said Eddie. "Just keep steering. Trouble is there are tons of feeder creeks and ditches. He could have stashed it in any—"

Off in a stand of cattails behind a low bank, Eddie spotted a dark shape.

"Hey," he said, raising the paddle. "What's that?"

Briggs poked his glasses to his nose and peered ahead.

"It's . . . I don't know what your skiff looks like, but that sure looks like some kind of small craft."

Eddie paddled the boat around the bank. The low dark profile of his skiff came into view, its proud up-swept prow poking out from freshly cut reeds.

He sat back, waving at the flies. The boat drifted past the skiff. It nosed into the grass and muck of the bank beside it and stopped with a gulp.

He turned to Briggs with a grin.

"Finest kind," he said. "We found the skiff."

"Finest kind?" said Briggs, blinking at Eddie through his glasses.

"Term in the fish business. Means the best, top quality. People around here use it all the time."

"*Finest kind*," said Briggs, smiling.

Eddie shook his head and grinned.

"Can't believe it. There are actually words you don't know."

CHAPTER SEVEN
AUGUST 12, 9:27 A.M.

EDDIE AND BRIGGS RODE in the skiff, towing the catboat behind them. The engine putt-putted with a steady cadence as they wound their way back out the creek. When the open water of the cove appeared ahead, Eddie eased back on the throttle.

"Do you think you should speed things up?" said Briggs, casting a look around the cove. "Jake might have come back, and I'm not sure he'd be overjoyed to see the two of us."

Eddie looked at Briggs. He saw him squint through his glasses, scanning the water ahead. Briggs started whistling, the same notes that Eddie heard in the Gut.

"Nervous?" said Eddie.

"Nervous?" said Briggs. "No, *nervous* is not the term I'd use. The term I'd use would be *petrified*."

"Well, whistling won't help. Besides, I told you Jake isn't the way you're making him out to be."

Briggs glanced at Eddie.

"Anyone associated with Marty has got to have evil cells in his bloodstream."

They left the cover of the marsh and the shanty came into view. Eddie saw *Nuthin's Easy* riding on her mooring out in the cove.

The skiff nosed into the open water.

The shanty and the walkway were empty, and the gull had returned to its perch on the rooftop.

"What a sec," said Eddie. "Where's the inflatable?"

He jerked his head around to see it burst from behind *Nuthin's Easy* on a course straight for them.

"*It's Jake!*" he said, wrenching the throttle as high as it would go. He steered toward the cove entrance.

"Oh, my," said Briggs, sinking down on the deck. "We're trapped."

Eddie glanced behind him to see the inflatable gaining fast.

"It's no use," he said. "Catboat's holding us back."

"Should we cut it loose?" said Briggs. His hair fluttered over his glasses. "We don't need it, do we?"

"Too late," said Eddie. He throttled back as Jake's inflatable sliced around in front of the skiff's bow. He looked at his hand. It was quivering. He felt as though he couldn't catch his breath.

Jake slowed down but the inflatable delivered a bump to the skiff that jolted Eddie and Briggs.

"What the hell are you trying to pull, Eddie?" said Jake, leaning over to grab the skiff's rail.

"Nothing," said Eddie. He heard his voice waver. He found himself pressed against the far rail, away from Jake. "Trying to get my skiff back."

"You think you know what the score is?" said Jake, glaring at Eddie. "You don't."

Eddie heard the first few notes of the aimless whistling coming from Briggs. Briggs's eyes met his. He looked helpless—Eddie knew exactly how he felt.

Jake rocked with the inflatable as it rode alongside, the engine gargling as it idled.

"What were you doing out on Greenhead?" he said.

"Bassing," said Eddie. "You told me about it."

Jake closed his eyes for moment, then opened them. "What else did you see out there?"

"Why'd you take my skiff?" said Eddie. His pulse jumped.

Jake narrowed his eyes. For a moment, he stared at Eddie. Then he grinned.

"Okay," he said. "I don't need any more water rats complicating my life. I'm giving you a choice. Keep your mouth shut. About everything. Don't tell the police. Don't tell anyone . . . especially your sister. You keep this between us, nothing happens to you."

Eddie licked his lips.

"But if you breathe a word," said Jake, lowering his voice, "either of you . . ." He paused to slide his eyes to Briggs. "If you breathe one word to anybody, you'll be in a world of hurt." He looked back at Eddie. "I promise you that. So don't do anything, understand? Don't even think about going back out to Greenhead."

Don't you tell me what to do, Jake Daggett, thought Eddie, anger flickering within his fear.

He worked his jaw muscle as the feeling burned for release. *Those lobsters aren't yours*, he thought. *I'll go after them if I want.*

"You understand?" said Jake, his voice louder.

"Yeah," said Eddie, the sound of his voice thin through his clenched teeth.

Jake straightened up.

"Now get out of here," he said. "Don't let me see you again. And remember: Don't go anywhere near Greenhead."

He put his boot against the rail of the skiff and shoved off. He snapped the engine into gear and hit the throttle. The inflatable reared up and shot away, its engine wailing.

Eddie watched the inflatable sweep around the cove in a long curve.

"Okay," he said, easing the throttle higher. "We're out of here."

Briggs was staring at the inflatable as it tore a white wake around *Nuthin's Easy*.

"I may have been a tad too hasty," said Briggs, "when I vowed to help you get those lobsters back. Which, of course, is impossible given the unfolding circumstances."

Eddie throttled up more and steered for the cove entrance.

"We have to inform the police," said Briggs. "He threatened us with our lives. It's the only way out. Otherwise Jake, who appears to be quite serious about all this, will be happy to make good on his threat."

Eddie looked back to see the inflatable pull up to the dock in front of the shanty.

"All the more reason," said Eddie, looking back toward the cove entrance, "to get out to Greenhead as fast as we can."

He heard Briggs laugh.

"That's a good one," said Briggs. "You're kidding, of course. You're pulling my proverbial leg."

"Those lobsters don't belong to him. And I can't go to the police because of Laurie. So I have no choice, do I?"

"Choice? Of course you have a choice. You have a . . . wait a minute. Laurie. Who, may I ask, is Laurie?"

"My sister. She and Jake . . . well, they hang out together sometimes.

Eddie kept his eyes on the water ahead.

Briggs cleared his throat. "Is it possible that Laurie's somehow involved?"

"Possibly. I'm not sure. I mean it's possible. What were you saying about having a choice?"

"A choice. Yes. You have a choice between staying alive if you avoid the island, and meeting your demise if you don't."

"If it makes you feel any better, there's no way they'll go out there now. Jake can't risk being seen in *Nuthin's Easy* and Marty went to work. And after we get the lobsters, I'll take you to the mainland, just like I said. My dad will be back by then, and he'll figure out how to handle Jake."

He looked at Briggs.

"Okay?"

"I did not for a moment believe," said Briggs, sighing, "that spending a summer at sailing camp would involve risking my life on a moment-by-moment basis."

Eddie smiled.

"So you're still in?"

"Let me be blunt," said Briggs, pushing his glasses back into position. "I am helping against my will, though I realize what I stand to gain. Quid pro quo."

"I help you," said Eddie, smiling, "you help me. Hold on. I'm going to see if we can get some more speed out of this old Evinrude."

He coaxed the throttle higher and the bow lifted.

"This is about as fast as we can go," he said over the engine whine, the air rushing in his face. "Keep an eye on the catboat, okay?"

Briggs looked back.

"Seems to be riding fine," he said.

Eddie weaved through the cove entrance and steered the skiff along the beach, skirting shoals and rocks jutting out of the water.

Over the buzz of the outboard Eddie heard a drumming sound. He scanned the sky, shading his eyes with his hand.

Above the point of land where the sailboats were, he spotted a speck hovering.

"Look at that," he said, pointing. "It's a Coast Guard helicopter. Now they're searching for you for sure. And over there on the water, it's their UTB."

Briggs pulled himself upright and peered at the speck, then out at the water.

"Do you really think," he said, "that my prison camp called the Coast Guard to look for me? And what is a *UTB*?"

Eddie looked at Briggs. "A utility boat. Out of the Fog Island Coast Guard Station. About forty-one foot and fast as anything on the water. We've seen it when we're out working gear. And why wouldn't they look for you? You're missing, and you're one of theirs."

Briggs smiled.

"No, I'm not one of theirs. They called the Coast Guard because they want their boat back."

Eddie looked at the speck.

"I guarantee they're after you," he said. "Kid goes missing at a camp like Saggy Neck and everyone's searching. Everyone on Fog Island will know about it in minutes."

Briggs snorted. "I suppose I had to disappear before Mr. Kendrick would do anything for me."

"All I know is we better get your boat hidden fast. If that helicopter comes any nearer, they'll spot us for sure."

Briggs stared at it.

"I do not want to be caught," he said.

"First thing we need is more gas," said Eddie. "Means we have stop back at our dock. We need a tarp for the lobsters, too."

"What if someone's there?"

Eddie glanced at his watch.

"Shouldn't be," said Eddie. "My mom and dad are still off-island, and Laurie's already at work. It'll just take us a minute. We can hide your boat there before we head out to Greenhead."

Briggs lifted his glasses up and kneaded the bridge of his nose.

"And afterward it's off to the mainland," he said, replacing his glasses, "just as we planned. Right?"

"That's the plan," said Eddie. "Look. See that point of land ahead, where those three pines are? Our cove's just around the other side. Now hold on. Let's see if we can squeeze even more out of her."

Chapter Eight

THEY PLANED AROUND the point close to the beach. The skiff's wake splashed ashore, flushing a flock of sanderlings. The birds circled and landed in the same spot as the waves moved on. Then Eddie throttled back to ease into the cove. They idled along the smooth water till the stack of lobster traps came into view. Eddie sized up the dock.

"Everything looks clear," he said, throttling up to gain more headway.

He ran his eyes from the water to the shore. A flicker's manic laugh echoed in the trees. On a bough of a dead pine tree overhanging the water, a kingfisher chattered. In the marsh beyond he heard ducks gabbling.

"See the marsh?" said Eddie as they slipped through the water. "That's where we'll hide your boat on our way out."

"You may not be aware of this, Eddie," said Briggs, "but you're beginning to think as deviously as Jake."

Eddie looked at him. "You gotta think like a thief to foil a thief," he said, grinning.

They neared the dock, the catboat gliding along behind them.

"Okay," said Eddie. "I'm going to bring us up on the starboard side . . . wait a minute . . ."

He looked toward the far end of the dock. Where the dock joined the sand driveway, someone was sitting in a beach chair.

"Who . . . who's that?" said Briggs. "There's a . . . a woman sitting in a chair."

"That's my sister," said Eddie. "What's she doing here?"

"What . . . I thought you said . . . what are you . . . what are we . . . what can we possibly do . . . what are we going to say . . . ?"

"Don't panic," said Eddie. "Listen. I've got an idea. Just play along, okay? And no whistling."

Briggs stared at the dock.

"Briggs, do you hear me?" said Eddie. "You have to play along."

Briggs looked at Eddie. "Okay," he said. "I'll try."

"Get ready to jump. And keep the boat from hitting the dock."

Eddie slowed the engine to an idle and the skiff drifted toward the dock. Briggs began whistling. Eddie frowned at him. The whistling stopped.

"All right," said Eddie. "Go ahead."

Briggs gathered himself, then jumped out, thumped

onto the rough boards, stumbled, and turned around to hold the skiff from the dock with his hand.

Eddie tossed him a line. Briggs dropped it, then picked it up. He blew his hair out of his face.

"Now what?" he said.

"Make it fast to that cleat," said Eddie.

Eddie put his foot out to keep the sailboat from bumping into the stern as it rode up behind the skiff. Then he climbed onto the dock.

When he turned around, he saw Laurie walking along the dock toward him. She wore rolled-up fatigues and a gray T-shirt reading "Fog Island Trap Co." She slid her sunglasses onto the top of her head. She held a paperback in one hand, her finger marking her place.

"What do we say?" said Briggs under his breath. "What are you going to tell her? What if she's in with Jake and Marty and tells them about . . ."

"Quiet," said Eddie.

"Hey, there," said Laurie. "I see you listened to Mom and stayed off the water. What time did you go out?"

Eddie shrugged. "Early."

Laurie sighed. "I just thought you'd like to know that I covered for you. Mom called early this morning and wanted to talk to you but I told her you'd gone over to Jerry's."

"Oh," said Eddie. "Thanks. How's Dad?"

"They were just heading to the hospital. The

procedure got moved back or something. Who's this?" she said, nodding toward Briggs.

"This is Briggs," said Eddie, "from the sailing camp."

"Pleased to meet you," said Briggs, extending his hand. "Briggs Fairfield."

Laurie smirked and shook his hand.

"Well, you don't get manners like that on Fog Island every day," she said.

"May I ask what book you're reading?" said Briggs.

Eddie forced himself not to shoot him a look.

She laughed and held it up. "It's *The Outermost House*, by Henry Beston. I've read it a couple of times."

"As have I," said Briggs. "I actually have a copy of it back at camp."

Eddie watched her expression change. Her smile faded and a baffled expression replaced it as she looked at Briggs.

She looked at the catboat, then back at Briggs.

"Wait a minute. Are you that kid who . . . I heard a call go out from the Coast Guard on the radio. They said a twelve-and-half-foot catboat piloted by a kid is reported missing from Saggy Neck. They're starting a search."

She nodded at the sailboat.

"Now that looks like a twelve-and-half-foot catboat to me. Are you—?"

"Yup, that's him," Eddie said. He did not need to look

at Briggs to know that he was blinking at him, about to say something.

"It's just a misunderstanding," he said before Briggs opened his mouth. "Yeah, we saw the Coast Guard boat and the helicopter out toward Saggy Neck. Kind of over- kill considering what really happened."

He laughed and looked at Briggs. "See what a mess you made of everything? All because of a little leak in the boat."

Briggs blinked at Eddie and opened his mouth. It hung slack for a moment, then snapped shut. He turned to Laurie.

"Yes, I did have trouble with the boat," he said. "I hap- pened to go out early this morning, before everyone else, and I found myself by Greenhead Island."

Eddie sneaked a look at Laurie to see if she reacted to the name of the island. But she was listening to Briggs without a change of expression.

"I must have hit a rock or something out there," said Briggs, "because I got a leak in the hull. I couldn't bail fast enough to keep up, and that's when your brother happened by."

"Wait a minute," said Laurie to Briggs. "What did you say you were you doing out by Greenhead Island?"

Eddie squatted to retie the bow line. He held his breath. Maybe she did know something about the lobsters.

Eddie forced himself not to look at Briggs.

"An early sail," said Briggs. Eddie fiddled with the

line. He heard the water lapping around the pilings. The kingfisher called.

"I happen to love single-handing a sailboat," said Briggs. "And I took the boat out early. I suppose it wasn't a bright thing to do. Especially considering the trouble I got into. And caused, it seems."

Eddie ventured a look up at his sister. She was considering Briggs through narrowed eyes. Had Briggs convinced her? Did she know about the lobsters?

She laughed.

"I can't believe they even got the Coast Guard out looking for you," she said. "But it sounds like you were lucky you didn't sink."

Eddie let out a thin stream of breath. She bought the story, it seemed.

Briggs grinned. "You're right. I bailed as much as I could, and then when Eddie said to get into his skiff, I discovered something else."

He paused and smiled at Laurie. He kept smiling but said nothing.

He looked back at Eddie.

"What did I discover?" Briggs said, his smile fading.

Don't push it, thought Eddie. *Now's the time to finish the story and shut up.*

Laurie blinked at him.

In a moment Briggs's smile beamed on strong.

"Oh, yeah! The minute I stepped out of my boat into Eddie's skiff the leak stopped. Just my weight in the boat was enough to cause the water to flow in. So the boat was fine, absolutely fine without me in it when we towed it here."

"Okay," said Laurie. She looked at Eddie. "So why did you tow the boat here instead of back to camp?"

"I was running low on gas," said Eddie, standing up. "Are you going to work today?"

Laurie groaned.

"Thanks for reminding me. I was just catching some sun before I go back to ice-cream hell."

"If you don't like it there," said Eddie, "why don't you go back to work for Dad?"

"As Dad himself would say, there's no percentage in it anymore."

"I don't think he really means it," said Eddie. "And he's hurt that you won't help."

She sighed. "I know. But working on that boat is a dead end. I could get trapped into working on it forever."

Eddie shrugged. "It's not forever. It would only be for a while, till Dad gets better. You'd help Mom out, too. You're going off to college, anyway."

"If I can afford it," she said. "Why do you think I'm working so much? Fog Island is a dead end for me. Unlike you, Mr. Lobsterman."

Eddie saw her smile at him.

Eddie looked at her. "I won't be one if the lobsters keep disappearing."

He watched her to see if he could read her expression.

"I know it," she said, shaking her head and looking out at the water. "Losing the lobsters is killing Dad."

He couldn't be sure about Laurie. Her reaction revealed nothing to him.

"He sure hasn't had any luck lately," said Eddie. "Did Mom say when they'd be home?"

"Too early to know. Maybe tonight, maybe tomorrow. Are you going to give Briggs a tow back to camp?"

"Yeah," said Eddie. "Something like that."

"Well, you better come right back afterward. Mom would scream if she knew I let you head out. To Greenhead Island no less."

"How late you working?"

"Not sure. They might want me to work an extra shift. Jake said he's thinking about heading out bassing again tonight. He's been out every night. Been skunked every time. Nada. So, if you want, I can come home on my break to make you some dinner."

Eddie made an effort not to look at Briggs.

"Don't worry about it," said Eddie.

"Hey," said Laurie. "I just thought of something. I'll bet the *Gazette* is going to interview you when they hear you found the missing kid and delivered him back to the sailing camp."

Eddie looked at her.

"What?"

"You saved Briggs. Maybe they'll even put you on TV. You're going to be famous. My little brother, the hero of Fog Island."

He said nothing. She had no way of knowing that returning Briggs to camp was not part of the plan.

Laurie looked at her watch, then up at the house.

"Where is he? I'm supposed to be at work by ten."

"Where's who?" said Eddie.

"Jake," said Laurie. "He's giving me a lift. If he ever shows up."

Eddie and Briggs glanced at each other.

"What's wrong with your car?" said Eddie, edging down the dock.

"Nothing," said Laurie. "I let Jake borrow it. His pickup conked out again."

"Ah, we better get moving," said Briggs. "I don't want to cause all the counselors and kids at camp any more worry than I already have."

Laurie pulled her cell phone out of her pocket and flipped it open.

"You're right," she said. "Maybe we should call Chief Snow right now to tell him that you found the missing kid."

"Laurie, don't," said Eddie, taking a step toward her. The thought that he could tell her he found the lobsters flashed into his mind. But he hesitated. She could still have something to do with it.

He saw her look at him.

"It's just . . . believe it or not," he said, "it would mean more to me if you let me tow him back to camp myself. If you call, then they'll already know, and . . ."

She snapped the phone closed and laughed.

"I'd ruin your moment of glory, right?" she said.

"Something like that."

"Okay," she said. "But you better get him back fast. You know how people get themselves worked up about stuff like this."

"I just have to grab the gas can," said Eddie, already walking down the dock toward the house. "Briggs, throw my boots in the skiff, would you?"

"It was nice to have met you," said Briggs to Laurie, extending his hand again.

Laurie smiled. "Same to you," she said, taking it. "Glad you're not missing anymore."

She slid her sunglasses on and went back to her chair. She opened her book and crossed her legs. Then she laid her book over the arm of the chair and pulled out her phone. She entered a number and put the phone to her ear, then snapped the phone closed and picked up her book again.

Eddie walked back from the shanty with a dented red metal gas can in one hand and a rolled-up tarp under his other arm. He quick-stepped past Laurie.

Without lifting her eyes, Laurie said, "Where you going with that?"

"With what?" he said, moving down the dock.

"The tarp."

"It's for the leak," he said, setting the gas can into the skiff and tossing the tarp in after it. "Let's go, Briggs. Gotta hurry."

Laurie adjusted her sunglasses. She looked at Eddie for a moment and closed her book. She picked up her phone again.

"Where is he?" she said to herself as she put her phone to her ear.

"Cast off," hissed Eddie as he yanked the starter. A cloud of blue smoke puffed out. The engine caught, sputtered, and fell dead. Briggs jumped to the cleat and fumbled with the line. Again the engine caught for a moment before it revved and fell dead.

"Come on," said Eddie, glancing up toward the house.

He tried again. This time the engine caught. Eddie looked up as Briggs tossed the line into the skiff and stepped aboard. Laurie looked toward the skiff.

"See ya, Laurie," called Eddie.

He guided the skiff into a turn and watched the towline go taut as the sailboat trailed behind them.

Laurie lifted her arm in a long, slow wave. As the skiff gained speed, her figure began to recede.

Then, over the sound of the engine, Eddie heard a car horn blare.

Eddie looked up toward the house. Laurie's car rolled to a stop beside it.

"It's Jake!" he said, ducking down, then peering over the rail behind them.

He saw Laurie get out of her chair and walk up the dock. When she stepped onto the sand lane, she broke into a trot toward the house.

"He might not see us," said Briggs, crouching low.

"Come on, Evinrude," said Eddie. "Get us out of here."

"What are we going to do with the catboat?"

"Can't leave it here now. We'll have to think of something else."

CHAPTER NINE

EDDIE KEPT THE THROTTLE wide open, steering the skiff through the royal blue water toward Tern Island, a scrap of marsh and beach and scrub lying dead ahead. Sheets of spray shot away from the bow. The catboat danced behind, cutting back and forth on the line. Questions came at Eddie as fast as the waves.

Should I have told Laurie about Jake? Is Jake going to tell Marty he saw us? Should I have told Laurie to call the police? Did she believe the story about Briggs, and is she going to tell Jake about it? Is she mixed up in the whole thing?

"Eddie?" said Briggs over the whine of the engine, his hair flattened by the wind. "What did you think of the yarn I spun back at the dock? Finest kind?"

Eddie glanced at him.

"Finest kind? Sounds like something I'd say."

"I know," said Briggs. "And you know something? Have you heard the way I've started talking?"

"What do you mean?"

"I'm doing it again. I just realized it myself."

"What are you talking about?"

"My habit of mimicking. I'm starting to talk like you."

Eddie shook his head.

"Do me a favor, will you?"

"What's that?"

"Be yourself."

Briggs blinked at him. "All right. So what did you think about my tall tale?"

"You mean about the leak?" said Eddie. "Not bad. You followed my lead just right. But it was pretty lame when you forgot what you were going to say."

"Pressure of the moment. And I was attempting to observe your sister's reaction to seeing you under surprising circumstances. I'm no Sherlock Holmes, but I was able to draw some conclusions from our interaction."

Eddie looked at Briggs. He had to admit that Briggs *was* irritating sometimes. The incessant chatter, the big words, the theories, the constant fiddling with his glasses, the gooney lanyard attached to them . . . it could get on your nerves, especially when you had to move fast, had no time to think of what to do.

Eddie surveyed the shore of the island. He spotted a place that looked good for hiding the catboat.

"Hold that thought," he said. "We're almost there. I need you to go forward and jump out to keep us off the rocks when we land."

"Will do," said Briggs, getting up. He made his way forward.

Eddie eased back on the throttle as they approached the shoreline.

"Okay," he said. "Get ready to jump."

Briggs placed one foot on the rail and leaned forward, gripping the rail with one hand to balance himself.

"Right," he said. "Tell me when. Wait."

He reached into his shorts pocket and pulled out his cell phone.

"What about this?"

"Give it to me," said Eddie. He took it and slipped it into the tackle box.

He glanced over the side at the bottom to see ridged white sand, patches of seaweed, and scattered rocks.

"Okay," he said. "Go ahead."

Briggs said "Geronimo!" and leaped, splashing into the shallows. He slipped on a rock and fell sideways into the water, pushing the skiff off the rocks with his feet.

Eddie cut the engine. He heard Briggs laugh.

"Not exactly finest kind," said Briggs, standing up in the knee-deep water to guide the skiff toward a small stretch of sand between the rocks. Water dripped off his glasses. "But at least I didn't take my phone for a dip."

"Better hurry," said Eddie, climbing out of the skiff.

"Run ahead to that marsh around the point and start pulling up some reeds. We have to cover the catboat."

"Okay," said Briggs, splashing ahead. "They should be as tall as I can find, yes?"

"Yeah."

Eddie beached the skiff, then untied the towline and hauled the catboat behind him. He waded around a rocky point, the catboat bobbing after him. He scanned the water between Tern Island and Fog Island. The sailboats off Saggy Neck were the only boats in sight.

When he brought the boat into the shallows, Briggs had already gathered an armful of long stalks.

"We'll have to take the mast down," said Eddie. "It'll show above the reeds if we don't."

"Unstep the mast," said Briggs, squinting upward. "I believe that's the proper terminology."

"Okay," said Eddie. "Let's get moving."

He leaned backward to tug on the line, drawing the catboat deep into the reeds.

"I'm . . . I'm afraid I don't quite know how to unstep the mast," said Briggs, "even though I know the term. I imagine we'll have to start with that." He pointed at the forestay and the turnbuckle that held it fast to the prow.

"Just keep gathering up reeds," said Eddie. "I'll take care of the mast."

He stripped off the black tape around the turnbuckle. The nuts were already loose, and when he twisted the turnbuckle, it spun free fast. The wire forestay went slack. With his jackknife he pried out the cotter pins and released the stay. He went around to the side and hauled himself onto the foredeck. He took the mast in both hands and lifted up with a grunt, working it back and forth until it popped free from its hole in the deck.

The mast began leaning over, and Eddie struggled to balance it. The gaff, boom, and sail, still attached to the mast, began swinging in different directions. He staggered, trying to get them under control, then recovered his balance, and muscled them into the cockpit.

Briggs returned with another armload of reeds. He was panting.

"I'm soaked, fly-bitten, and nearly exhausted," he said. "But somehow I'm exhilarated. I feel as if we were engaged in some sort of elaborate escapade, a daring escape from a penal colony. Did you ever hear of Papillon? He was a . . ."

"Hand those to me," said Eddie.

He reached down as Briggs passed the armload of reeds to him.

"So what was it?" he said. "Your observation."

He began spreading the reeds out on the foredeck.

Briggs cleared his throat. "My conclusion may not be accurate," he said.

Eddie took the last of the reeds from Briggs.

"Briggs," said Eddie. "Spit it out."

Briggs brushed his hands together as he looked up at Eddie.

"I simply want to say that after observing your sister back at the dock," he said, "I wasn't convinced that she's involved with Jake and Marty."

Eddie stopped. He looked down at Briggs.

He wished he had drawn the same conclusion—and that he could stop the suspicion she was involved from gnawing away at him.

Briggs raised a hand.

"It might be little more than a gut feeling," he said. "But she doesn't appear to have the same hard heart that Jake has. Marty has no heart at all, of course."

Eddie looked out at the water.

"I hope you're right," he said. "But after what Marty said about needing her for something, and what Jake said about not telling her anything, I don't know. I tried to get a reaction out of her but I couldn't tell."

"Might Jake have said that because he wanted to play you?"

"It's possible. But why would Laurie have asked you what you were doing out by Greenhead?"

Eddie looked back at Briggs.

Briggs frowned.

"As I mentioned," he said, "my theory is not based on hard facts."

Eddie spread the last of the reeds over the cockpit.

"We better get moving," he said. "I hope you're right. But we can't be sure."

He stepped over the boom and readied himself to climb off the boat.

Would Jake have been able to do any of this without Laurie knowing? he wondered, easing himself over the side into the water. *To steal the lobsters right from the end of our own dock?*

He didn't want to believe it, but she had to have known.

Chapter Ten

THE SKIFF PLANED across the bay, reaching hull speed now without the burden of the catboat.

"I can imagine that you're torn," said Briggs. "But how can you lay your suspicions to rest without coming out and asking her?"

Eddie shrugged. "If she's involved, and I ask her, and she knows we know, what kind of a bind will that put us in?"

Eddie stared out at the horizon. Maybe Laurie hadn't really gone as far as stealing lobsters with Jake and Marty. Still, she could have tipped Jake off without realizing it. Eddie's dad had been out on a two-day trip the night the lobsters disappeared from the lobster car. The lobsters were moving to deeper water as the weather got cooler, and he was shifting gear to follow them. Had Laurie mentioned to Jake that Dad would be gone? But that was the kind of news that traveled fast on Fog Island, so Jake could have heard about it from anyone.

But why had Marty and Jake talked about her as if she were part of the plot?

"Eddie, do you see that?" said Briggs, pointing. "Coming toward us where the other boats are?"

Eddie looked across the water. Coming toward them was a red-hulled powerboat.

"Hey," said Eddie. "Looks like he's heading right for us."

He watched the boat.

"And he's really moving, too," he said. "I don't think we can outrun him."

Briggs stared across the water at the boat. A frown crossed his face.

"I know that boat. It's the committee boat from the camp, the one they always use to put out the markers when we race."

"Well, it's definitely gaining on us."

Briggs sank down and shook his head.

"I can't believe this. They're going to catch me before I have a chance to make my escape. I'll be back facing Marty before we even have a chance to get the lobsters back."

Eddie looked at him. He felt a pang of guilt that he'd thought Briggs was irritating. Here he was, someone he'd only met hours ago, now willing to risk his neck to help him get his father's lobsters back.

"Don't give up yet," said Eddie. "Stay low. Maybe we can make it into Greenhead Gut. They might not follow."

Briggs slid his legs beneath the seat and squirmed flat.

"This okay?" he said.

Eddie glanced at him.

"For now."

He scanned the water ahead. The water looked smooth right up to Greenhead Island.

"I forgot something," he said. "Tide's not right. It's almost slack tide. The Gut won't be making." He peered beyond the Gut, where the break to the ocean lay.

"But there's a big marsh out that way," he said, "out by the barrier beach before the ocean. Maybe we can make it there and hide."

Briggs peered over the rail.

"I think it's too late," he said. He reached down for the tarp. "I'll have to cover myself with this."

"Hurry," said Eddie, looking back at the boat.

Briggs stretched out on the bottom of the skiff and drew the tarp over him.

Eddie saw someone on the boat step up on the deck by the pilothouse and beckon toward him.

"And remember to keep quiet," he said to Briggs, "if you can."

Briggs was silent for a moment. Then, his voice muffled by the tarp, he said, "Eddie, I resent that."

"Be quiet," said Eddie. "They're signaling us to stop."

"What's that smell?" said Briggs.

"What smell?"

"That stench. Enveloping me. And there are flakes falling on me."

"It's bait, old bait, old, rotten bait, and old fish scales, and if you don't shut up, they're going to catch you."

"If I don't suffocate first."

"Briggs!" hissed Eddie. "Pull your feet in. Your shoes are sticking out. And don't say another word, or I'll take you back to camp myself."

"Okay," said Briggs. "I promise. Not another word."

Eddie shook his head as he watched the red boat cruise across the water toward them, churning out a white bow wave. He could hear the throb of its engine as it drew closer. The person on the deck motioned for Eddie to slow down. Eddie glanced toward the marsh, but it was too far away for him to chance a run.

He heard the red boat's engine throttle down. He eased off the throttle of the outboard.

"What's going on?" said Briggs.

"Quiet," said Eddie. "They're coming alongside."

The boat idled up to the skiff. Its wake rolled underneath the hull, and the skiff rocked hard. In the pilothouse, an older man stood at the helm.

"Hey, kid," yelled the person who had been waving. He lurched across the deck and leaned on the rail.

Eddie looked up at him. His heart blinked. It was

Marty. A shiver swarmed up his neck and spread across his cheeks.

"You see any catboats out this way?" said Marty over the grumble of the engine. He narrowed his eyes and tucked a hank of hair behind his ear.

Eddie shook his head. He wasn't sure he could make his tongue work.

"Nope," he said, taking off his cap and running his hand over his hair. "I haven't seen anything, except those boats over there." He pointed toward Saggy Neck and tugged the cap back down on his head.

Marty gripped the rail and leaned forward, eyeing Eddie and the skiff. Eddie eased the skiff away as the boats bobbed on the small waves.

"You sure?" called Marty. "A little catboat? Tall kid with glasses sailing it? He stole the boat, and we want it back—and we want the kid back, too."

He looked at Eddie.

"But hey," he said. "Don't I know you from some-place?"

Eddie could not breathe.

"Beats me," he said. "Is that what the helicopter's looking for? The kid in the catboat?"

The man at the helm stuck his head out the pilot-house door. He had cropped gray hair and a white long-sleeve T-shirt that read "Saggy Neck Sailing Camp."

"Let's go, Marty," he said. "We've got a lot of water to cover."

"Okay," said Marty. "Hey, kid. If you see anything, call the camp. Got it?"

He looked at Eddie for a long moment. His eyes narrowed again.

Eddie nodded and stopped himself from twisting the throttle and rocketing off as fast as he could. Instead, he let the skiff drift while the red boat turned. He made himself look busy by filling the engine with gas from the gas can.

He glanced up. On the afterdeck of the red boat he saw Marty staring at him as the boat throttled up and powered away.

"Don't move," he said to Briggs between clenched teeth. He topped off the engine and set the gas can back on the deck. "He's still watching us."

"Eddie, I have to tell you something," said Briggs.

"Wait till they're gone. I'm going slow. I don't want him seeing us heading out to Greenhead."

"I am about to die from asphyxiation," said Briggs, his voice thin. "Do you think he knew I was under here?"

"Yeah," said Eddie. "He saw right through the tarp. Of course not, but he could ruin everything for us anyway. He must have recognized me."

"The reek in here is almost too much to bear."

"Just hold on. They're heading away fast. But I think we're sunk."

"Sunk? I am the one who is sunk. If Marty comes back for me, he will grab me by the scruff of my neck, cackle his evil wheezing laugh, and throw me to the sharks, and not even Mr. Kendrick will dare stop him."

"Mr. Kendrick?"

"Remember? The head of the camp. That was him. The man at the helm. He would no more help save me from Marty now than he did back at camp."

"Marty didn't know you were there. But he's got to know who I am."

After a moment, Briggs said, "Marty might be mean, but he's not that bright. Wasn't it dark when he saw your skiff on the island?"

"Yeah, but . . ."

"How well do you know him?"

"Not that well. I've seen him hanging around with Jake. But he's got to know me."

"I'm sure he thinks your skiff is still in the marsh. Jake couldn't have told him or he would have made the connection."

Eddie looked back across the water. The red boat was slicing toward the horizon, on a course for Saggy Neck and the small sailboats.

"Maybe Jake didn't say anything to him," he said, "because he's trying to protect Laurie. But if he didn't say anything to Marty, does that mean Laurie's involved or not?"

He shook his head. "At least we know one thing. Laurie didn't call the police or anyone or they would have had a description of my skiff."

"Eddie?" said Briggs.

Eddie looked down at the tarp. Briggs's shoes were sticking out from underneath it.

"What?"

Briggs cleared his throat.

"May I come out now?"

CHAPTER ELEVEN
AUGUST 12, 12:36 P.M.

BRIGGS WAS STILL PLUCKING fish scales out of his hair and flicking the silvery disks overboard when Eddie slowed to bring the skiff toward the beach near the tidal pool.

"Better keep our eyes open for rocks and snags," said Eddie.

He idled the skiff through the shallows, easing his way around a line of exposed rocks.

"So we're going to grab the lobsters and run, right?" said Briggs, rubbing his palms together. "Make short work of it?"

"That's the idea. I'll bring us along the beach here and get as close to the tidal pool as I can."

"Eddie, wait a second," said Briggs. "I think I hear something. Someone's out here. A boat. Is that Jake and Marty's boat?"

Eddie throttled up and brought the skiff around.

"No time to find out," said Eddie. "Could be. Or it

could be someone searching for you. But we've got to get out of here." He looked back toward the sound. A point of land blocked his view. "We better find out if other boats are out here before we get the lobsters. Let's go around to the other side."

"Perfect," said Briggs, "So much for going after the lobsters right away."

"Got to be smart about this," he said. "Anyone could see us loading up or hauling the lobsters back home. Someone looking for you, like the Coast Guard, could show up here anytime. There's no telling. I think we can get a good look at the top of the island. We don't want to blow it now when we're so close."

"What if that's Jake and Marty?"

Eddie scanned the water ahead, then back where he'd heard the boat. It was still hidden by the point. He saw Briggs blinking at him through his glasses. He couldn't let Briggs exasperate him—not now.

"I don't think they'd make their move yet," he said at last. "They don't want to be seen, either. Besides, Marty's probably still on the committee boat."

Briggs scratched his cheek. "But they might be desperate," he said, "especially if Marty recognized you. He'll probably tell Jake they have to take all the lobsters now. That might be Jake behind us."

"If Marty recognized me," said Eddie, "what's he going to do? He's trapped on the committee boat with someone from camp. He can't exactly say, 'I'm off with Jake to get the lobsters we stole,' can he?"

"Anything could happen. Marty could drop Kendrick off at camp. He could take the boat back here himself. He could pick up Jake. You have to agree, Eddie, that in circumstances such as these, bad things are bound to happen."

Eddie frowned at Briggs.

"You kill me, you know that?" he said, his irritation taking control. "You know what you are? You're a wimp. A skinny old wimp."

Briggs opened his mouth to say something, but then stopped. He blinked at Eddie.

Eddie shook his head.

"I don't know what's going to happen any more than you do," said Eddie. "But at least I keep my mouth shut about it."

He looked back at Briggs. He was cleaning his glasses on his shirt. His mouth was set in a line. When his eyes met Eddie's, he looked away.

Eddie lifted his cap and ran his hand through his hair. He let out a stream of breath.

"Aw, Briggs, listen. I'm sorry. I didn't mean it. Now I'm starting to sound like my dad when the lobstering's going lousy. See what happens when I open my mouth? I'm sorry. I really am."

Briggs replaced his glasses and looked out at the water. He sighed.

"I realize you're under a lot of pressure," he said, "to get your father's lobsters back, to avoid Jake and Marty. But I see no reason"—he reached down to pluck a fish scale off his knee—"I see no reason to take your anxieties out on your only ally."

Eddie throttled back and turned to Briggs.

"Fair enough," he said. "But you should try getting over it. The way you get yourself in a twist about every little thing."

Briggs sneaked a look at Eddie.

"You have to realize that I have always been expected to act older than my age. I suppose getting myself in a twist about every little thing is how this pressure manifests itself. And yet I demonstrate my immaturity, or, I should say, my actual age, in many ways."

"Briggs?" said Eddie.

"Yes?"

"Shut up."

Briggs blinked twice.

"Kidding," said Eddie, giving him a grin. "Now listen. Just around that sand spit should be the beach where I first saw you. Get ready to jump out."

"What about the boat that was following us?"

"If you were paying attention," said Eddie, "you would have seen it heading the other direction. It wasn't following us."

Briggs looked back.

"Ah, yes," he said.

Eddie brought the skiff around the sand spit and steered for the beach. He glanced over the side to see clumps of green eelgrass and ridged sand littered with shells through the shallow water.

"Ready?" he said.

"Ready, even though my boat shoes and socks will never be dry again."

Eddie cut the engine and let the skiff coast in. As soon as the keel scraped bottom, he told Briggs to jump. Then he followed and they grabbed the rails and hauled the boat up the strip of sand into the undergrowth.

"Let's get her farther up," he said. "On three. Ready?"

"Ready!"

"One, two . . ."

Briggs threw himself against the skiff with a grunt, then fell onto the sand when the skiff didn't budge.

"I said on three," said Eddie.

"Oh," said Briggs.

"I didn't say on two."

"Sorry. I guess I was too enthusiastic."

"Let's try it again."

They succeeded in shoving the skiff into the scrub till not even the prop on the outboard showed.

"We're going to head straight up through the woods to the top," said Eddie. He reached back into the tackle box for the sandwich and granola bar and stuffed them into his pocket. "No telling how long we'll be," he said. "Let's go."

"Okay," said Briggs. "All I need is a pith helmet and a blunderbuss."

Eddie moved off, ducking under branches, sidestepping holes and rocks and brambles. Briggs stuck close behind him.

Eddie worked his way up the hill. He shouldered through a screen of tall bushes, the branches raking his arms.

"Watch out," he said, turning around to wait on the other side. "These things have thorns."

He heard sticks snapping and branches shivering, and then Briggs burst out and crashed onto the ground, his glasses askew and twigs and leaves festooning his hair.

Eddie gripped Briggs by the arm and hauled him up.

"You okay?" he said.

Briggs adjusted his glasses.

"To tell you the truth," said Briggs, "I am the opposite of finest kind."

"Let's keep moving," said Eddie.

When they neared the peak of the island, Eddie could see the sky through the treetops, and soon they stepped into a small grassy clearing where only a scattering of locust trees grew, their pale green fringes of leaves waving against the blue. Grass covering the ground in heavy sweeps like an animal's pelt surrounded the boney trunks. Blueberry bushes crowded the edge of the clearing.

"This must be the highest point," said Eddie. "Look, you can see back across the bay to Fog Island and out beyond the break."

Briggs grasped his knees, panting. Then he straightened up, plucked a leaf from the temple of his glasses, and ran his wrist across his forehead.

Above, the leaves fluttered in the breeze, making a sound like a flowing stream.

Eddie shielded his eyes with his hand.

"You see that?" he said, "coming around the tide pool side of the island? It's the committee boat. And there's a bunch of other boats, too, coming toward the island. That must have been what that first boat was—someone searching for you."

"Not good," panted Briggs. "If Marty recognized you, maybe he trumped up an excuse to leave camp to come after you."

"Could be," said Eddie. "He might be part of a search party. But if they're all coming out to Greenhead to look for you, Marty can't do anything about the lobsters with the other boats around whether he recognized me or not."

He looked in the other direction.

Far out over the ocean, he saw a long black wall.

"Fog," he said. "Looks like it's rolling our way."

Briggs plucked a few blueberries from a branch.

"Are these edible?" he said. "Now that I think of it, I'm starving."

"Yeah, you can eat those. But here." He pulled the sandwich out of his pocket. "We'll split this."

He unwrapped the sandwich and handed half to Briggs.

"We even have dessert," he said, producing the granola bar and breaking it in half.

"Thanks, Eddie," said Briggs. "Never has such a frugal repast looked so appetizing."

They both chewed in silence, watching the boats patrolling. Eddie looked at Briggs. "When you were going to sail to the mainland," he said, munching, "had you figured out what you'd do if you'd made it?"

Briggs swallowed. "I hadn't really thought it out. I just wanted to escape and then find a way to get back home to Bedford Hills. But I guess there's really not much choice if you don't have money. Hitchhiking is the only way."

"I have to admit," said Eddie. "I can't really see you hitching. But if you want to try it once we get you over there, I won't stop you."

Briggs nodded. "I can't say I can picture myself hitch-hiking, either. But then I couldn't picture myself sailing through the Gut or racing around in a skiff, pursued by thieves. I must say I never would have thought I was capable of such exploits."

Briggs took a bite of his granola bar and chewed for a moment.

"A question I've never asked you," he said, "is what

are you going to do when you get the lobsters back? Are you going to tell the police about Jake and Marty then?"

"I don't know," said Eddie. "By that time, my mom and dad will be home. I'll have to tell them what happened. Dad might not even want to let Chief Snow know we got the lobsters back, especially if he finds out Laurie was involved."

Eddie finished chewing and wiped his hands on his jeans. He heard the breeze whisper in the leaves.

"The wind's shifted. Bet that fog moves in soon."

He peered through the trees to the water below.

"I can't believe this," he said. "You see that?"

Briggs pushed aside a branch and looked down.

"Yeah. What about it?"

"See the committee boat?" said Eddie. "That's got to be Marty. He's right off the tidal pool like he's guarding the lobsters or trying to block the view of the pool or something. And there are more boats out there now. That even looks like Chief Snow in his whaler."

The pale green leaves quivered. Above the trees, a plume of white vapor flew by.

"We're stuck," he said. "And it looks like the fog is coming sooner than later. Dad always says to stay off the water in a thick fog, if you have the choice. But I guess we don't. And right now we don't have any choice but to wait."

"Nobody will be able to get to the lobsters now," said Briggs. "Not even us."

Eddie squinted down at the red boat.

"Those boats can't stay out there forever," he said. "But if they take off before Marty"—he glanced at Briggs, then looked back—"we'll just have to be ready to make our move."

PART II

THE CATCH

CHAPTER TWELVE

THE WORLD WAS a dark pearl. In the distance, the Fog Island Light foghorn mooed every few seconds. Eddie leaned against a tree trunk, keeping watch, the fog churning past. He could only make out a smudge where the boat idled off the tidal pool. The burble of the engine came to him through the fog, now softer, now louder, as the boat shifted position. The other boats had gradually moved away, disappearing into the fog.

"This is killing me," he said. "I can't keep waiting like this."

Briggs was sitting cross-legged with his back against a tree, weaving blades of grass together.

He looked up at Eddie. "I know what you mean. I wish I had my guitar. Playing makes the time vanish."

Eddie yawned and stretched out on the grass.

"He can't stay there much longer," he said, staring up into the grayness. He checked his watch. "It's about twenty past seven now, and he's got to head back sooner or later to meet Jake for the last job."

"How long have we been waiting?" said Briggs.

"Since about one, one-thirty."

"What do you think your father will say," said Briggs, "when he sees his lobsters again?"

Eddie smiled.

"I don't know. He probably won't say a word but weigh his share, load them up, and take them over to the co-op to sell them. No questions asked."

"Sounds a bit like my father," said Briggs. "'Never apologize, never explain' is the motto of a gentleman."

From the direction of the tidal pool, Eddie heard the boat engine rumble louder.

He popped up and peered through the fog.

"This is it," he said. "He's taking off. Let's get moving."

Briggs sighed.

"For a moment," he said, picking himself up and letting the grass blades flutter to the ground, "I forgot why we were here."

Eddie plunged into the undergrowth, Briggs on his heels. They crashed through thickets and raced through stands of scrub oaks and pitch pines. At last they broke onto the beach where they'd hidden the skiff. They launched it and weaved their way around rocks and shoals as they made their way back to the tidal pool.

Eddie and Briggs hauled the skiff to the beach. "Keep your eyes and ears open. No telling who might show up."

They ran to the tidal pool and looked in.

"Amazing," said Briggs. "How many of them do you think there are?"

In their crates the lobsters felt their way over each other. Their green and black mottled backs glistened in the dimming fog-filtered light.

"I don't know how deep this pool is," said Eddie. "Just right here there must be about ten crates, and they're full. So I'd bet there's a good thousand pounds just on the top."

They reached in and hefted the first crate to the lip of the pool, then dragged it to the skiff. Eddie unlatched the door and began setting the lobsters two at a time into the bottom.

"How come you're doing that?" said Briggs. "Why don't we just take the crates?"

"We can fit more this way," said Eddie. "We'll fill up the skiff, unload them, and come back on another run."

"We haven't even completed this run," said Briggs. "I'd call this only half a heist."

Eddie reached down to lift two more lobsters out of the crate. The thought struck him that if Jake and Marty came back, they'd realize some of the lobsters were missing. But what other choice did he have? He had to take the risk.

He set the lobsters in the skiff and straightened up to look at Briggs, who stood aside, rubbing his chin.

"Uh, aren't you going to help?"

Briggs nodded. "Of course. Just as soon as I figure out how. You have to understand that I am not used to handling live animals."

"Briggs, we don't have time for this. Watch me. They can't get you because they're banded."

Eddie grabbed another one and held it up for Briggs to see.

"Get them right around the back. Nothing to it. The soft ones are shedders. That's how they grow, by shedding their shells. We usually catch more during the shed. Not this year, though."

Briggs cleared his throat. He inched his hand toward one, then grabbed it. Before he could lift it up, the lobster flapped its tail, and Briggs jerked his hand away.

"Don't say anything, please," he said. "I flinched, that's all. Now I have a better feel for it. That was only a trial run."

He eased his hand down and took hold of a lobster. Keeping it at arm's length, he stepped to the skiff and set it in.

"At this rate," said Eddie, "we can get Marty and Jake to help us load up."

Briggs raised his eyebrows. "Very well. I know a challenge when I hear one."

He leaned over and grabbed the last two lobsters out of the crate and plopped them in the skiff. He turned toward Eddie, brushing his hands together.

"There," he said.

"That's more like it. Okay. Let's move."

They hauled two more crates, huffing and gasping as they hefted each one over to the skiff.

After they set the lobsters into the bottom, they hid the empty crates in the undergrowth.

"That'll do it," said Eddie, straightening up and wiping his forehead. He checked his watch. "Took longer than I thought. I'll cover them with the tarp. We need to keep them wet on the ride back."

They pushed the skiff into the water and jumped in. Eddie started the outboard.

"I've got to go slow," he said as the skiff eased ahead. "See how low we are in the water?" He felt the sluggishness of the skiff as they idled away. "This is more than a full load. I don't want us capsizing or taking sea over the rail. Hold on."

As they rounded the last point, they pushed into the waves, a small choppy sea kicked up by the damp breeze.

The fog swallowed them. Ahead was a blank gray wall.

"Eddie," said Briggs, his voice quiet. "How can we be sure we're heading in the right direction? We're losing the light, too."

"I took a bearing when we passed that last point," said Eddie. "And I can still hear the foghorn. I'll use that to be sure we're on course."

Briggs took off his glasses and wiped them on his shirt.

"The fog's so thick it's beading up on my glasses," he said. "You must have a sixth sense to see through it."

The Fog Island horn sounded over the low hum of the engine.

"Long as I hear that," said Eddie, "we should be okay. Nothing to do with a sixth sense."

They fell silent as they crept into the deepening gloom. The skiff rocked harder. Briggs gripped the rail with both hands. Now and then spray splattered them as the boat smacked through a wave.

Eddie heard the sound of the aimless whistle.

"Briggs," said Eddie, "you're whistling."

"Oh," he said, glancing around him. "Sorry. I guess not being able to see where we're going unnerves me a bit."

Enveloped in fog, the skiff seemed to be moving on the same small rough disk of water.

He needs something to do, thought Eddie, *to take his mind off things.*

"Okay," said Eddie. "Reach over easy and get some water in the bucket. Have to keep the bugs wet."

Briggs stood up and grasped the bucket. He went to the rail and eased the bucket downward till it caught the water flowing past. When it caught the water, it jerked him backward, and he staggered, then regained his balance.

"That was almost the end of me," he said as he lifted it up. "Where should I pour it?"

Eddie reached out and patted the tarp. He could feel the lobsters moving underneath.

"Just a little here," he said.

Briggs splashed half the bucket over the tarp.

"That'll do it," said Eddie. "Don't want to swamp the boat. She's leaky enough as it is."

"Eddie," said Briggs. "Just a moment. Do you hear that? It sounds like the motor of a boat."

Eddie throttled back. The skiff slowed, bobbing on the waves.

"Yeah," he said. "It's coming from over there. Out beyond the Gut."

He throttled up and turned the skiff away from the sound.

"I can still hear it," said Briggs. "It's getting closer."

The skiff shuddered as it hit a bigger wave.

"Hold on," said Eddie.

"Eddie," said Briggs, "I think it's heading right for us."

Eddie squinted into the fog. He could hear the boat, but he could see nothing.

"Okay," he said. "I've got to speed up. Hang on."

He throttled up. The skiff's stern settled deeper into the water and the bow strained to lift.

"Now it's even closer," said Briggs, his voice sounding tight. "I think they're on a collision course with us."

The skiff pounded into a wave and heeled. Eddie could feel the weight of the lobsters sliding and shifting and pushing the boat over.

"I think we're in the Gut now," he said, straining to bring the skiff back on course.

109

"The boat," said Briggs, his voice tight, "I think the boat's right over there."

Eddie felt the throb of an engine closing toward them. He squinted to see where the boat was. He brought the skiff around just as he heard the churning slosh of a bow wave and saw a form loom out of the fog in front of them.

He turned hard and saw the hull of a fishing boat. The skiff scraped and banged against it.

"Whoa!" said Briggs, reaching for the rail as the skiff tipped. "We're going over!"

Eddie looked up at the hull as it pushed past to see the name *Nuthin's Easy* under the flare of the bow.

Then the skiff lifted. He grabbed for the lobsters as the tarp pulled free. The skiff heeled over hard, teetering on the crest of a wave, sending lobsters tumbling into the water. Eddie felt himself growing lighter as the skiff began to capsize.

CHAPTER THIRTEEN

THE SKIFF CLUNG to the crest of the wave, its starboard side nearly upright. Eddie shot his hand out to grab the rail, trying to offset the motion of the boat before it flipped. At that moment another wave surged underneath them from the opposite direction. It swept under the skiff's port side, shoving it level. Eddie grabbed the tarp and pulled it back aboard. The pulse of the engine drew away from them in the fog. Eddie throttled down and the skiff bucked on the chop.

"What just happened?" said Briggs. "Did we just get run down? Did we almost capsize?"

"I don't know," said Eddie. "They either didn't see us or they tried to ram us. My guess is from the course they were on that it was Jake heading to town to pick up Marty. We better get these lobsters home."

He checked his watch: 8:14. He calculated when they

would spot Tern Island light. Judging from how long they had been going since they left Greenhead Island, it would be in about ten minutes.

"Did we lose a lot of lobsters?" said Briggs.

"Still have most of them."

"Eddie?" said Briggs.

"What?"

"I've been thinking," said Briggs. "What if the police catch Jake and Marty when they're taking the entire load of lobsters to their rendezvous point? That way all the thieves will be caught. Maybe we need to let the police know where the lobsters are, even if it does mean jeopardizing Laurie."

"We've been through this," said Eddie. "It's too much of a risk to Laurie. It's not what my dad would do."

"I don't know," said Briggs. "I'm beginning to wonder if it's too much of a risk to our lives if we don't."

"We'll be all right," said Eddie. "Just hold on tight and keep your eyes open. Ready?"

Briggs cleared his throat.

"I'm clutching the rail for dear life, if that's what you mean."

"Okay. Here we go."

Eddie twisted the throttle and the skiff shouldered forward. He squinted into the wall of fog and listened for the foghorn. At the top of a wave he heard the moaning call. It was closer now: a good sign.

"Keep your eyes dead ahead," he said. "We should be

getting near the Tern Island channel marker. Keep your eyes open for a flash of light."

They pushed through the fog, the hull slapping against the chop. Eddie squinted ahead, knowing that the visibility would only worsen with the deepening darkness.

"Hey, Briggs," he said. "I think we've found something that keeps you from talking so much."

"What makes you think I'm not talking? I'm just not doing it out loud."

Eddie tried to see through the gloom. He knew they were close to the buoy. But still he saw only blankness as they pushed through the water.

"Wait a second," said Briggs. "Right over there. I think I saw something."

Eddie throttled back and checked his watch again: 8:24. Ten minutes on the nose.

"Look," said Briggs, his voice rising. "There it is again, a red glow. Just for a second."

Out of the fog a blurry reddish pulse of light appeared for moment, then vanished.

"There it is," said Eddie. "That's the channel marker by Tern Island."

He brought the skiff around to point at the light and throttled up as high as he could. The skiff cut over a swell, then dipped down. Spray splashed over them.

"Hang on," said Eddie. "There's still a good sea running. It must be coming through the break."

Soon the flashing red light grew more distinct in the gloom. Eddie kept the throttle wide open. As they passed the light, Eddie brought the skiff around in a slow curve. They bounded over a wave and slapped down so hard the skiff quivered.

"Not too far now," he said.

Soon the red flash diminished behind them and Eddie throttled back.

"You hear anything, Briggs?" said Eddie.

"Only the engine," he said, "and the desperate drumbeat of my heart."

"Listen for waves breaking," said Eddie. "That way we can tell if we're near Tern Island."

The skiff wallowed over the swells as they cruised along at half speed.

"I can't believe we found the channel marker," said Briggs. "You must be used to doing this kind of thing."

"Used to what?"

"Cruising around in a tiny boat completely blind."

Eddie laughed with relief. "Not on purpose. But I've been caught in a thick fog before, mostly when I've been working on my dad's boat. This stuff is getting pretty thick, but when we've been offshore it was even thicker. You toss a stone overboard, it disappears before it hits the water."

"I don't know about you," said Briggs, "but I feel like I should have my hands out in front of me, the way you do when you're trying to feel your way down a dark hallway.

You just know you're going to trip over something, but you don't know when."

"Don't worry," said Eddie. "Once we're past Tern Island, we're home free."

Eddie tilted his head, straining to hear over the engine. He turned toward a hissing sound in the distance.

"That's waves breaking way over there. Must be Tern Island."

He eased back on the throttle. "I've got to slow down. We'll be on shore in minutes."

For a moment, another light appeared ahead of them. It glowed yellow in the darkness.

"Hey, see that light over there?" said Eddie. "Must be Ryder's place. I know exactly where we are now."

"You mean to tell me," said Briggs, "that you didn't know exactly where we were before?"

Eddie revved the engine again.

"I knew where we were, but not the whole time. You have go by feel."

Eddie fixed his eyes ahead, watching for any variation in the grayness. Off to port, he made out the darker shape of the shoreline.

"We're coming into the mouth of the cove now," he said.

Through the fog, Eddie made out the faint glow of the light at the end of his father's dock.

"We're almost there," he said. "Let's make this quick."

They idled toward the dock and came into the circle

of light above the lobster car. Fog swirled through the floodlight.

"My parents didn't make it home yet," said Eddie, nodding at the dock. "*Marie A.* isn't back."

He maneuvered the skiff to the dock and Briggs jumped out with a line and cleated it off.

"It's good to be able to see again," he said, "and to feel solid ground."

"When we head back," said Eddie. "You can take a turn steering the skiff."

"You're kidding me, right?"

"You're catching on."

Eddie jumped out and went over to the car. He kneeled down and opened the top of the cage.

"Okay," he said, walking back. "I wish we could dump them right in from the skiff but I can't get it over there. Grab one of those bins and we'll fill it up with them."

Briggs lifted a plastic bin off a stack and slid it over to the skiff.

They reached over the skiff's rail and began plucking lobsters out of the bottom and setting them into the bin.

"They're still in good shape," said Eddie. "Be careful you don't get yourself stuck by a spine."

"I know just how you feel, Mr. Lobster," said Briggs, holding one up. Its feelers waggled in the light and it snapped its tail to try to escape. "Flailing around and not getting anywhere."

"Actually, that's a female," said Eddie. "See the two

thin things underneath, like feelers? A male's are thicker and jointed, like this one."

"Ah, I do see. I never knew that."

"You'll be a pro at this before you know it," said Eddie. "Now let's get them into the water."

They slid the bin across the dock, hoisted it up a step to get it onto the main dock, then set it at the end by the car.

They lifted lobsters out of the bin two by two and dropped them into the water.

"We'll probably only have two or three crates to empty," said Eddie. "We must have lost about a hundred pounds of them when we nearly tipped over. That's about half of a good day's catch right there."

Soon they were unloading the last crate. Briggs grabbed two lobsters and plopped them into the water.

He straightened up and stretched his back.

"This is more work than I've done in . . ." he said, twisting at the waist, "than I've done in my entire life."

"This is it," said Eddie, picking up the last two lobsters and dropping them into the water.

"Wait a minute," said Briggs, looking up the dock toward the house. "I just saw lights. Up there. Look."

Headlights swept through the fog and flared on the side of the house. Car tires crackled on the driveway.

The headlights washed over them, switched to high, and froze them in the beam.

"Oh, man," said Eddie. "It's a cop car."

A spotlight arrowed out from the cruiser as it rumbled down to the dock and entered the circle of light. They were trapped in the spotlight.

"Gotta get out of here," said Eddie.

"Hey, you!" The driver threw open the door and pushed his way out. He broke into a run and thumped onto the dock.

Eddie bounded out of the spotlight and jumped into the skiff. He glanced back to see Chief Snow lumbering down the dock, his mustache white in the glare of the light.

"You there!" called Chief Snow. "Freeze! Freeze or I'll shoot!"

Chapter Fourteen

August 12, 9:45 p.m.

The outboard wailed to life. Briggs leaped from the dock and plunged onto the tarp as Eddie goosed the throttle. The prop bit into the water and the skiff swerved away.

Eddie looked back to see Chief Snow pounding down the dock planks, the fog swirling past him under the light.

"Get down," said Eddie.

"I'm not getting underneath that tarp," said Briggs, "if it's the last . . ."

Eddie looked back to see Chief Snow stop at the edge of the dock.

"I think he's going to shoot. Down! Now!"

Briggs yanked the tarp over him and burrowed beneath it.

"*Eddie?*" At the sound of his name, Eddie looked back

at the dock. Could Chief Snow have recognized him even in the fog and the dark? Had he recognized his skiff?

"*Eddie Atwell, get back here right now!*" Eddie heard Chief Snow yell over the outboard. He saw him raise his arm. The fog swirled, closing over the dock and turning it into a diminishing blur.

"I can't believe this," said Briggs, his voice muffled. "He's trying to kill us."

Eddie bent low and looked forward to check their heading. In the rush he thought Chief Snow was going to use his gun, but now he realized that he was only waving. His heart was stuttering in his chest just the same.

"*We were almost shot!*" said Briggs, his breathing coming fast. "Shot at point-blank range! Eddie, we were almost gunned down."

"He didn't even pull his gun. Saw it was my skiff and held off."

Briggs pushed the tarp off him and sat up.

"So," said Briggs, "if he wasn't going to shoot us, why did we take off? Maybe we should have just told Chief Snow everything. Maybe we should have let him know that we were putting lobsters back in and about the lobsters on Greenhead Island."

"And what if Laurie's messed up in this?" said Eddie, a spark of anger flaring in his belly. "Did you forget that part? You want me to send my own sister up the creek?"

"Eddie," said Briggs after a minute. "I didn't mean to anger you. I only posed the question."

Eddie stared ahead. His anger cooled, but he kept turning over in his mind that he had just run from the police. What had Briggs said? "Bad things are bound to happen." He was dead right about that.

They rounded the point into the open channel. Eddie picked up Tern Island light's faint glow and steered for it. The cove disappeared in the fog and darkness behind them.

"We've got to stay ahead of Chief Snow," he said. "He'll be after us in the police whaler before you know it. And then there's *Nuthin's Easy*."

"My nemesis on one side of us," said Briggs, "police on the other. And now we're heading back into the fog."

"I know where we're going," said Eddie. "I got us back before."

"Never had a gun aimed at me," said Briggs. "My hands are still shaking."

"No one fired a shot," said Eddie.

"Eddie, Chief Snow must think we're the thieves. Or performing a copycat crime. He wanted to gun us down."

"Enough, Briggs. Did you hear a pistol go off? No. We weren't shot. So stop talking about it."

The skiff bounced along the water.

"The only course of action, then," said Briggs, "is to go to the police to clear ourselves. You have to see the logic of that."

Eddie clenched his jaw.

"Out of the question."

Briggs sighed.

"Somehow I had a feeling you'd say that. And if we keep trying to elude Chief Snow, we'll make it even harder on ourselves if we're caught. So what do you think about trying a different tack? If we had solid evidence against Jake and Marty, then we could clear everything up, even if something goes wrong."

Eddie glanced at Briggs. "Evidence against Jake and Marty?" he said. "Yeah, we could use that. The problem is how to get it. And I have no idea."

"For once I do," he said, pointing at the tackle box. "My phone has a camera. What if we get a picture of them in the act? A picture of them that would implicate them and clear us? I would love nothing more than to bring Marty to justice. You said they were going to hit another place tonight before going to the mainland."

"Two places," said Eddie. "Philbrick's and Crossman's. Philbrick's is just to the west of here. Crossman's is way on the other side of the island. They didn't say when they were going, but they'll have to hit them soon if they're going to make the mainland before light."

"If we could get a picture, we could get it to the police. And you wouldn't even have to have your name attached to it. So you wouldn't have to violate the code you live by."

"Code?"

"This streak of obstinate Yankee independence. This code of the lobsterman."

"It's not just that," said Eddie. "It's Laurie, too. But it seems like a long shot."

"I see no other way to clear ourselves unless we lure the police to catch Marty and Jake in the act. But that seems impossible."

"Just how we can pull it off is the question. And I can't let it stop us from getting more lobsters. That means more to me than putting Jake and Marty behind bars."

"But what happens," said Briggs, "if we're behind bars?"

Eddie felt his stomach clench—not from hunger. What would his dad do if he weren't hobbled by his shoulder? Could he be sure his father wouldn't go to the police right away if he knew who the thieves were? Was Laurie the only reason he didn't want to go to the police? Ratting out Jake—an islander—was still ratting. But now he wasn't so sure trying to do everything alone made sense.

He glanced at Briggs. Maybe he was right. If they could get the evidence to the police right away, they might still have time to go back for more lobsters.

"I guess it's worth a try," he said. "But they might not even show up. Who knows if their plans have changed."

"Not seeing Marty ever again would be a blessing," said Briggs, sighing. "Though if we don't encounter him again, nothing will be solved. We would be left in the bind we're in now."

"Let's do it," said Eddie, bringing the bow of the skiff

around on a different heading. "It's taking a big chance, but it could work."

"But if it doesn't work . . ."

"If it doesn't," said Eddie, "you'll just have to be ready to use your fists."

"My what?"

"Your fists. The only way we'll be able to get a shot of them while they're stealing the lobsters is to be right up close, practically on top of them. Find a hiding place. If they see us, we'll have to be ready to take them on."

"*Take them on.* Suddenly this seems like a very bad idea. I would have been better off holding my tongue."

"See that light ahead?" said Eddie. "The red flash? That's the entrance to Philbrick's cove."

"I have a confession to make, Eddie," said Briggs. "I have never in my span of years been involved in a rumble."

"A rumble?"

"A brawl."

"Don't worry. With any luck, they won't even know we're there."

"Luck," said Briggs, "seems to be in somewhat short supply."

The flashing red light grew more distinct in the darkness and fog, and soon Eddie steered the skiff past the breakwater and inside the cove entrance. He throttled back. The skiff creased the smooth water. Ahead, he made out a cone of light above a dock.

"Philbrick's put up a light just like my father did," he

said. "His boat's there, too. It's tied up on the other side of the dock."

"Do you think Marty and Jake will be bold enough to try to steal lobsters with the victim's boat right there?"

"They did when our boat was," said Eddie. "They know even lobstermen have to sleep sometimes. Better be quiet. Tide's low so we might be able to get underneath the dock."

"I'm not sure about this," said Briggs.

"I'm not sure, either," said Eddie. "But you better get your phone ready to take a picture."

Eddie cut the engine and the skiff drifted toward the dock. He took the phone out of the tackle box and handed it to Briggs.

"I'm not sure about this," said Briggs.

"You said that."

"My nerves," said Briggs, "have stunned my tongue."

"Keep it down," said Eddie, reaching out to push the skiff off a piling. "And remember not to whistle. Who knows if Philbrick is around? We have to get as near to the lobster car as we can."

Eddie lowered his head as the skiff passed between two pilings and slid beneath the dock. In the cavernlike space, the lapping of the water echoed and the glare from the spotlight fell in stripes through the gaps between the dock planks above. Eddie spotted a wooden ladder that reached from the dock into the water.

"Hold on," he whispered. "You hear that?"

"What?"

"Coming in the cove. A boat."

"*Nuthin's Easy*?"

"Probably. Got to move fast. I'm going to climb up underneath the dock here in the beams. You take the skiff around the other side of Philbrick's boat. Give me the phone."

"It's all set to take a picture," said Briggs, handing it back. "All you have to do is press that."

"Got it. Steady the boat while I climb up."

Eddie pocketed the phone and reached up to the ladder. He set his foot on a rung and pulled himself off the boat, then waved at Briggs.

"Just stay out of sight," he whispered.

Briggs pushed off as Eddie climbed up the ladder. The sound of the motor approaching grew louder.

This is going to be tricky, he thought, reaching up to the crossbeam that formed a ledge at the end of the dock. He laid both hands on the ledge and swung one leg up and pulled his body flat onto the narrow shelf just as a fluttering commotion swept past his face. He flinched and he lost his balance and gripped the edge of the beam to keep himself from tumbling into the water.

He glanced down at the water moving below him. He heard the echoing lap of the waves against the pilings. From above, slants of light slicing through the dock planks glinted on the surface.

Gasping, he hauled himself back up.

126

Pigeon, he thought, feeling his hands tremble from the exertion of pulling himself up. The clap of wings receded, then returned as the bird landed at the opposite end of the ledge. It began cooing.

Eddie pulled in his breath as he settled himself on the ledge. The lobster car lay just beyond his perch beneath the dock, bathed in bright light. He reached into his pocket and eased the phone toward his chest.

The boat idled toward the lobster car and swung the stern around to it, then cut its engine. Eddie still heard the pigeon cooing along with thumps coming from the boat. He leaned over the ledge to peek. In the strong light, he glimpsed the name *Nuthin's Easy* on the stern pressed against the lobster car. From his angled view, he saw Jake leaning over to begin the transfer.

Better not wait, he thought, easing the phone downward. He craned his head around once more to gauge the correct angle.

How much noise does this thing make? he wondered. He laid his finger against the button, then lowered the phone to the spot he estimated would be level with the boat's name. Water splashed and a bang sounded on the boat. He pressed down and the pigeon cooed at the same time that the camera clicked. He pulled the phone back up.

That better have worked, he thought, his chest thudding. Another bang came from the boat followed by more splashes.

Not very quiet. Bound to wake up Philbrick. It's a wonder they haven't been caught by now.

Then the boat engine grated to life and *Nuthin's Easy* mumbled away into the darkness.

Eddie waited till the engine was only a murmur toward the cove entrance before he dangled his foot to feel for the rungs of the ladder. He climbed down as Briggs brought the skiff back to meet him.

"Got it," said Eddie, stepping onto the skiff. He handed the phone back to Briggs as he took the throttle. "Take a look."

The pigeon cooed again.

Eddie looked up.

"Thanks, bird," he said. "Thanks for covering for me."

CHAPTER FIFTEEN
AUGUST 12, 10:27 P.M.

"**SHOWS THE NAME** of *Nuthin's Easy* as clear as day," said Briggs, looking at the screen of the phone. "And the lobster car is in the frame, too. I must commend you on your bravery, Eddie."

"Hardly," he said. "That pigeon scared me so much I almost fell into the water."

Eddie steered the skiff past the flashing red light at the cove entrance into open water.

"If the police see that it's *Nuthin's Easy*," said Briggs, "they might not even suspect Laurie. If she's involved, that is. The faster we get the picture to the police, the better, I say."

Eddie peered ahead. The skiff rocked over the small chop. They had the evidence, true. But getting it to the police could wait. He knew what he had to do: Go get more lobsters. Trying to clear themselves would come later.

"We're going to take the shortcut around the other

side of Tern Island," he said, throttling up higher. "We're heading back out to Greenhead. Then we'll get the picture to the police."

Eddie waited. He knew Briggs was priming himself to speak. He turned to look at him. Briggs was cleaning his glasses.

"I am not," said Briggs finally, looking up, "in favor of this strategy."

"One more load," said Eddie. "If we don't, we could lose our chance to get any more at all. Even if Marty and Jake are heading over to Crossman's, we're not going to have enough time to get back home, print out the picture, take it to the police, and go out for another load. Besides, we got lucky at Philbrick's, and one thing I know is that luck doesn't last."

"On the contrary, Eddie, our luck seems to have changed, and we should consider involving the police sooner rather than later. Do you know what would have happened had Marty and Jake spotted you taking a picture of their—"

A jolt shot through the skiff, cutting Briggs off. The skiff jerked sideways as if a giant fist had punched the hull from below, and it bucked upward, the engine racing.

We must have hit a rock was Eddie's first thought as he began a slow backward somersault off the stern of the boat. Out of the corner of his eye, he saw Briggs vanish overboard.

Eddie flipped past the engine. He seemed to be

moving in his sleep, as if he were someone else watching Eddie Atwell somersaulting overboard. He felt his cap fly off just before he hit the water and plummeted past the whirring propeller of the engine. The water was cold and black as he sank down deep. Underwater the outboard made a gurgling whine as the skiff headed away. He kicked and flailed, clawing for the surface, his lungs bursting and burning. He broke into the air, gasping. He heard the engine but he could not see the boat. He coughed and gagged and spat out seawater as he fought to keep his head above the surface.

I'm going to die, he thought. *I'm sinking.*

The water kept washing over his face and gagging him. He could not stay at the surface.

My boots, he thought.

His boots were filled with water, heavy enough to pull him under.

He sucked in a deep breath and brought one foot up toward him. He sank as he worked the boot loose. As soon as it slipped off, it dropped away into the blackness. He kicked to the surface for another breath, then brought the other foot up and pried the boot off.

He shot to the surface and sucked in air. He coughed, spat, and breathed in again. Free of his boots, he was more buoyant, and he could keep his chin above the water. He heard the outboard in the distance.

"Briggs!" he yelled. "Briggs, where are you?"

He spat out seawater again.

"Briggs!" he called. "Answer me!"

He heard the engine in the darkness. Was it getting closer? Was that possible? He bobbed on the small waves.

"Briggs!" he called. "Briggs, where are you?"

The engine sound was definitely getting closer.

"Eddie!" came Briggs's voice. "Over here!"

Eddie couldn't tell how far away he was.

"Briggs!" he yelled. "I'll keep calling to you. Swim toward my voice."

"Eddie," called Briggs. "The skiff. I think it's heading back toward me."

Eddie realized that he must have bumped the handle of the engine and shoved it to the side when he went overboard, sending the skiff off on a long turn. The skiff was running in a circle with no one aboard.

"Eddie, it's coming closer. I think it's heading right . . . I can't really see . . ."

"Briggs, hold on, don't . . ."

There was a loud thump and the sound of the engine continued on its way.

"BRIGGS!" he yelled, breast-stroking as hard as he could toward the sound. "Briggs, where are you?"

He pictured the skiff coming around in a circle. Briggs wouldn't have been able to see it coming. It would have been on him before he could swim out of its path.

If he had been hit by the skiff . . .

"BRIGGS!" yelled Eddie, his voice cracking. His breathing came fast. "Answer me, Briggs!"

He kept swimming in the blackness.

"Oh my God," said Eddie. "Oh my God." He choked on the water. He gagged and spat.

My fault. So what if I timed it right to Tern Island Light? Big deal. Pure luck. Now I'm paying for it. And Briggs is, too.

He heard the engine coming closer again. At first he thought he had to get out of the skiff's way, but then another idea came to him.

If he could get on the skiff, he'd have the flashlight, and he could find Briggs.

He began taking steady strokes toward the sound.

The engine sound came closer.

He arms weakened. He dog-paddled toward it.

One chance, he thought. *After that, don't know what I'll do.*

The sound grew louder. He stopped swimming and started treading water.

There it is, he thought. He could hear the engine and the water splashing past the bow. It was almost on him.

Then it was there and the hull hit him. He tumbled past it and he reached his arm up, clawing at the side. He slipped past and spun and reached up again and grasped on to the stern rail right beside the engine. The skiff dragged him through the water and he thought he couldn't hold on as the water pulled at him. He could feel the prop churn out a pulse of water right beside his waist. The prop would chop him to ribbons if he got tangled up with it.

Then he slammed his other hand onto the rail and reached up for the kill switch on the engine. He plucked the cord with the tip of his fingers but it slipped away. His arm was beginning to quiver and he thought he was going to have to drop back, but he heaved himself forward and clutched the cord and tugged.

The engine coughed and went dead.

For a moment he hung off the stern of the skiff, his chest heaving, his lungs on fire. The skiff bobbed on the water, small waves lapping at the hull. The sound of the foghorn came to him.

Can't wait, he thought.

He hauled himself into the skiff. He grabbed the starter and pulled and the engine whined to life. He fumbled for the flashlight, found it, and switched it on.

Water was gathering around his feet.

A hole, he thought. *Whatever we hit caused a leak. A fast one.*

"BRIGGS!" he yelled over the sound of the engine as he idled back toward where he thought he had last heard him.

He trained the flashlight on the water, sweeping it back and forth.

All he saw were small waves coming at him from the fog. He switched the beam of the flashlight back into the bottom of the skiff to search for the leak.

Water bubbled in fast.

He kept calling as he steered the skiff back and forth and swept the water with the beam of the flashlight.

He realized that he had to get to shore to fix the leak before he could continue looking for Briggs, but he didn't want to leave.

He knew if he left, Briggs was done.

He'd been knocked out, Eddie was sure, but maybe he had come to. What if he had a concussion and was disoriented? He could never swim to Tern Island. There was no way he could swim in the right direction. He might be treading water, only shouting distance from the skiff.

But the skiff was sinking. He had no choice. He had to make the run ashore.

CHAPTER SIXTEEN

AUGUST 12, 10:56 P.M.

EDDIE BROUGHT THE THROTTLE up as high as he could so the skiff's bow would lift. The leak slowed as the skiff planed over the water.

It's all my fault, he thought, scanning the water ahead, his hand feeling weak as he gripped the throttle. *It's not bad luck. It's just my fault. I let us head too far to the west, into the rocks. Should have known better. Bad decision. Should have taken the picture in first. Shouldn't have let this happen. Should have listened to him.*

Briggs. Gone.

He spotted the glow of Tern Island Light and brought the skiff toward it. He was closer to Tern Island than he'd thought.

Better see how far it is, he thought. He slowed the engine to listen.

At first he heard only the splash of water against the

hull. Then, over the mumble of the idling engine, he heard the wash of small waves.

He switched on his flashlight and pointed it at the shore, catching the sudsy back of a wave running up on the beach. He revved the engine up to gain headway, then cut it. The skiff coasted through the water, swayed on the waves, then ground to a stop on the sand.

He jumped out and hauled the skiff above the surf.

Move fast, he told himself. *Briggs doesn't have much time.*

Got to find a lever to flip the boat, he thought. He grabbed the flashlight and raked the woods with the beam, slashing it back and forth, looking for deadfall. All the limbs he saw were too small or too frail.

What's over the rise on the other side of the island? he thought. *Driftwood? A downed tree?* No time to find out. Anyway Briggs is on this side. In the water.

"BRIGGS!" he called out.

Got to find driftwood, he thought. He jogged along the beach, sweeping the beam back and forth as he went. Every few feet he stopped and called over the water for Briggs.

There, at the far point, he spotted a bough, bleached almost bone-white. He sprinted to it. The bough was half buried in the sand. He worked it back and forth till it loosened, then slid free.

He hefted it over his shoulder and jogged back to the skiff, calling out for Briggs as he went.

Dropping to his knees in front of the hull, he dug out

a small trench, then slid the bough into it. He levered it upward, the skiff rising as he pushed.

"Almost there," he gasped, his feet sliding backward in the sand, when the bough cracked. He tumbled backward as the skiff lumbered back to the sand with a boom.

Can't keep messing up like this. Got to get back out there.

He sat up.

"BRIGGS!" he yelled over the dark water.

He pulled himself to his hands and knees, panting.

I can't do this, he thought, his stomach swimming. *I'm done. Briggs is done for.*

He clenched his teeth and ground his eyes closed. He did not want to let the tears out. Anger seized him like a hot fist inside his chest.

Don't fall apart now. Get a grip. Figure out how to tip the skiff over some other way.

A sound came from the water—a sound different from the splash of the waves. At first he thought it could only be a sound the waves were making. But then he heard it again.

It was a kind of chirp.

It sounded like a songbird whistling an aimless tune.

He stood up. Was he hearing things?

But there it was again, a steady chirping, coming from the water.

"Briggs?" he called, switching on the flashlight. "Briggs, is that you out there?"

In the beam of the flashlight, he could see nothing but the small waves running in. The fog had pulled back. The chirping continued. It was louder now.

"BRIGGS!" he yelled. "Is that you?"

And then he saw a lighter spot in the flashlight beam, and a head bobbed into view just above the surface.

"BRIGGS!" he yelled, dropping the flashlight on the beach and racing into the water. He ran through the waves, the water rising up to his waist, and grabbed Briggs by his shirt.

"I've got you," he panted. "I've got you."

They stumbled through the water and fell down on the sand.

Briggs had stopped whistling and now he was panting.

"Good thing," he said between gasps, "good thing . . ."

"Catch your breath," said Eddie. "Don't talk."

Briggs lay on his back, huffing. Slowly his breathing returned to normal.

"It's a good thing," he said, "that my prison camp . . . that they made sure we could swim before we sailed. Those tortuous, cold, early morning lessons saved my life. That . . . that and your flashlight."

"My flashlight?"

"I could see it from the water, flashing back and forth. Just a blur. But it was there. And if I hadn't, if I hadn't seen it, I'd be swimming blind to Portugal right now."

He touched his hand to the bridge of his nose as if his glasses were still there. "Maybe you can tell me what happened," he said. "I was in the water before I could even take a breath."

"We hit a rock," said Eddie. "It was my fault. I brought us too far to the west, trying to make the shortcut around Tern Island."

"It was an accident. There's no need to flog yourself."

Eddie looked at Briggs. He was back. He'd thought he was dead but he was back. He was shivering, and he had lost his glasses, but he was back.

"The skiff tried to run me down," said Briggs. "It almost hit me, but I did a surface dive. After that I didn't know where I was, and when I called out for you, you didn't answer, even though I could hear you calling for me."

He reached into his pocket, then took his hand back out.

"I dare not even peek at what I am positive has become an iSponge," he said. "Our ploy to clear our names has been drowned along with it."

Eddie cleared his throat.

"And my Red Sox cap. I've had that for . . . but, Briggs. I thought you'd drowned."

Briggs looked up at him.

"Well, I'm alive. Half drowned, but alive. And, unfortunately, almost blind. And perhaps a degree away from hypothermia."

"Hang on a second," said Eddie. He went over to the skiff and pulled out the old sweatshirt he always kept under the midship seat.

"Put this on," he said, tossing it to Briggs. "Try to warm up."

Briggs sat up and peeled off his shirt. Then he forced himself into the sweatshirt.

"I have been likened to a stork before," he said, his wrists protruding from the sleeves, "because of the lanky nature of my frame, but this sweatshirt is most welcome."

Eddie looked at him. He was gawky and sopping and blind and shivering, but he was, thought Eddie, a sight for the proverbial sore eyes, as Briggs himself might have put it.

A picture of guiding Briggs by the elbow along the beach on Greenhead Island came to Eddie.

He sighed.

"I guess this is it."

Briggs peered up at him.

"What do you mean?"

"I mean, you almost drowned, and you don't have your glasses. The boat's shot. It's too much. Marty and Jake are out there somewhere. We can't go back to Greenhead for the lobsters."

He knew it was true. Briggs almost died. Going after the lobsters—and Jake and Marty—wasn't worth that.

"Eddie," said Briggs. "We made it this far, didn't we? We can still execute our plans."

"Briggs, you almost . . ."

"Eddie, listen. We're almost there. We can do what we

set out to do. Either that or forever regret allowing the opportunity to slip away."

He squinted toward the skiff, then opened his eyes wide and blinked.

"Though I'm not quite sure what good I'll be," he said, "groping around like a mole. And I can't envision how I'll fare hitchhiking without being able to see the road in front of me. I can only conclude that my part of the plan is out. But we still can execute your part, can we not?"

"Don't you have an extra pair or something?"

"In my duffel bag. Back at camp."

"Maybe we can figure out a way to get them."

"I don't know," said Briggs. "We should focus on the lobsters. And on how to bring Marty to justice. Jake, too, but especially Marty. My history with Marty, I must confess, has an even darker side. It was the reason I resorted to such desperate measures to escape."

Eddie saw Briggs sneak a look at him.

"Go ahead," said Eddie. "You can tell me."

Briggs sighed.

"Very well. I was heading to talent night as I was telling you before, if you remember, and Marty came up behind me. He was carrying some sailing gear—life jackets and a coil of line—and I tried to let him go by. But he dropped the gear and grabbed me. He said he was sick of rich 'punks,' especially one who thought he had any right to talk to his girlfriend. He pulled my guitar case out of my hand and threw it to the ground and jumped up and down on it like it was a trampoline. I loved that guitar. It was a Leo Kottke edition Taylor that my parents had bought for me when I was ten. I'd only had it for three years and every year it was getting better, more seasoned. But now it's a pile of splinters. I could only stand there. I couldn't move. But that wasn't the worst of it."

He paused, glanced at Eddie, then continued.

"He laughed at me. He laughed. And he said he was going to make my life miserable, and that he was going to enjoy every minute of it. And then . . ."

He paused. He cleared his throat.

". . . and then he threw me down and put his foot on my throat so I couldn't make a sound. He took the line he was carrying and pulled my arms behind me and lashed my wrists together—and then tied them to my ankles. I was trussed up like one of the calves I'd seen a cowboy rope at the dude ranch, worse than a lobster with bands on its claws."

Eddie stared at Briggs.

"I didn't move for a long time," said Briggs. "I didn't know what to do. I was sick to my stomach because I had submitted, submitted without a fight. But I was in luck, if luck is what you can call it. Everyone was at the talent show, so I wormed my way across the grounds to the dining cabin. The old gentleman who did odd jobs around the camp was out on the porch, sweeping up after dinner. He looked at me struggling across the dirt and sand and gravel, said, 'Stay put,' disappeared inside, and returned with a butcher knife. 'Some prank,' he said as he cut me free. 'Kids get more vicious every year.'"

Eddie pictured Briggs lying under the shrubs, his wrists tied to his feet.

"But we don't have to submit," said Briggs, his voice low. "We can still fight. Can't we?"

He's right, thought Eddie. *We can't quit now.* He knew they had to finish what they'd started. But could they really pull this off themselves? Briggs had nearly died. Who could they turn to for help, short of surrendering to Chief Snow?

"We're in way over our heads," said Eddie, "but yeah, we can still fight. Jake and Marty haven't won yet, have they? First we have to fix the skiff and get back out to Greenhead and get those lobsters before they do. And then we'll get you to the mainland, glasses or no glasses. You ready?"

Briggs pushed himself up to stand beside Eddie.

"Some exertion might warm me up," he said.

The mainland, thought Eddie. Maybe the mainland was the key. If they could find out where Jake and Marty were taking the lobsters, they could let Chief Snow know—and clear themselves.

"Might I ask how you managed to get the skiff back?" said Briggs.

"I got lucky," said Eddie. "Just like you." He laughed. "Hearing your crazy whistling out there was the best sound I've ever heard in my life."

"Eddie," said Briggs. "I am flattered that you would say such a thing."

He glanced at Briggs. In the darkness he could see him smile.

"Okay," said Eddie. "We better get going. Let's tip the boat up. Here, over this way. Can you see at all?"

"I can make out some shapes. Just point me in the right direction."

"Reach down and grab the rail."

"Okay."

They hefted the skiff onto its side.

"Hold it there," said Eddie, stooping to inspect the planks with his flashlight.

"That's where we hit," he said, running his hand along the rough wood. He poked a finger into the crack and wiggled it inside the boat.

"Broke right through," he said.

"I'd appreciate it," said Briggs through clenched teeth, "if you'd hurry. I'm going to drop the boat on my toes. Then I'll be blind and lame."

Eddie grabbed the rail and helped Briggs lower the skiff to the sand.

"We can plug it with a piece of the tarp," he said. "Just like caulking a seam."

Briggs held the flashlight as Eddie took out his jackknife and sliced a handkerchief-sized square out of the tarp. He rolled it up tight as a cigar. Then they lifted the boat on its side again. Eddie bent down and jammed the tube into the hole and tamped it in with a rock.

"Okay," he said. "Feels tight. Let's get her in the water."

Grabbing the rails, they slid the boat back into the small waves. Eddie climbed in and held his hand by the plug.

"Seems to be holding," he said as the boat rocked on the waves. "Only a little is seeping in. But it always did anyway. Even for Laurie."

Briggs cleared his throat.

"Eddie, you yourself said that we're in way over our heads. Don't you think the time has come for us to get some help?"

Eddie peered at him.

"What are you suggesting?"

"Laurie," said Briggs. "I am suggesting that we turn to Laurie. We have no other choice. And she's your sister. Even if she were involved—which, as I mentioned, I have grounds for doubting—wouldn't she help you? Blood being thicker than water, and all that?"

She could help, thought Eddie. She could get word to Chief Snow while he and Briggs found out where Jake and Marty were taking the lobsters—if she wasn't mixed up in everything. Would she really steal from her family just to make enough money to leave Fog Island? He thought of Briggs's gut feeling that she wasn't involved. She might have made the mistake of getting wrapped up with Jake in the first place, but she wouldn't hurt her own family, would she? How could he not trust her?

He didn't see any other choice. They had to take the chance.

He hadn't realized how much of a burden he had been carrying by suspecting his sister. Now the thought of turning to her for help buoyed him as if he had kicked off another pair of water-filled seaboots.

"You're right, Briggs," he said. "If we can find out where Jake and Marty are taking the lobsters on the mainland, we can expose the whole operation. But we need Laurie's help."

"Laurie's help," said Briggs. "That's what I was saying. Are you agreeing with me?"

"If we're going to get help from anybody," said Eddie, "it's going to be her. We just have to take the risk."

"I wish I could see the expression on your face," said Briggs, "to see if you're pulling my leg or not."

Out of the gloom on the other side of the island, a beam of light probed through the darkness and flashed along the beach.

"Somebody else," said Briggs, "seems to want to see your expression, too."

"We're out of here," said Eddie. "Stay close."

At that moment he heard Chief Snow's voice boom through a megaphone.

"Eddie Atwell, I know you're out there."

So he does think we're the thieves, thought Eddie.

"Give yourself up," the voice echoed through the night.

Chapter Seventeen

August 13, 12:02 a.m.

THEY RACED BACK to the skiff and shoved off. Eddie started the engine and ran the skiff close to the beach toward the far point, keeping the rise between them and the searchlight.

"Don't we want to get away from him," said Briggs, "now that there's no doubt in his mind we're the prime suspects?"

"If we head straight out," said Eddie, "he'll see us in the open water. Once we get to the point we'll be okay. Stay low."

When they neared the point, he looked behind the skiff to see the searchlight playing over the marsh.

"Good enough," he said. "Better make our move. He must be inspecting your boat. Hold on."

He brought the skiff around to head straight into the darkness and fog, revving the engine as high as it would go. Spray slashed over them as the skiff cut through the chop.

"If it was daylight out," he said, peering behind him, "they'd already have us."

"How'd they find us?"

"Logical place to start since he saw us heading out in this direction in the first place. Might have seen the light from the flashlight, too. We're going to have to find Laurie fast and get back out to Greenhead before Jake and Marty beat us to it."

"I don't know which is worse," said Briggs, hunching his back against the spray, "the prospect of facing Jake and Marty again or heading back into this maritime purgatory."

Soon the light at Ryder's place appeared through the fog, and they rounded the point into the cove. Ahead, the dock was empty.

"My dad's still not back," said Eddie, scanning the cove and the dock. He turned the skiff and ran the boat behind a low point straight into a smaller inlet. He cut the engine, and they drifted through a stand of reeds to a rocky beach.

"We'll hide the skiff here," he said. "Chief Snow might double back."

They jumped out and Eddie tied the skiff to a tree. They made their way up the slope through the woods. In his bare feet, Eddie took careful steps. He winced now and then when he stepped on a sharp twig or stone. But he had to almost laugh out loud when he thought of Briggs, who hadn't lost his boat shoes even though his eyeglasses had gone to the bottom—in spite of the lanyard.

"Eddie?"

Eddie turned around. Briggs wasn't behind him.

"Where are you?"

"Over here," said Briggs.

"Briggs," said Eddie. "Don't wander off. Come this way."

Briggs crunched through the undergrowth to join Eddie, and they hid behind the trunk of a tree. Eddie peered around it to scout out the situation.

The house stood just beyond the trees. An outside light shined on the grass of the back yard.

"Lights are on inside," said Eddie. "Somebody must be there."

"Laurie?"

"If it's not Laurie, I don't know who it is. My parents aren't home yet."

Could Jake be there? he thought. *He better not be.*

They crouched down while Eddie took a last look at the house.

"Okay, *now!*" he said, and they broke through the brush and sprinted across the lit yard, their shadows rippling with them over the coarse grass. They made it to the side of the house by the kitchen window and pressed their backs against the shingles. Eddie glanced at Briggs and put his finger to his lips. The window was open. Eddie smelled bacon frying.

"I told you, Mom," he heard Laurie saying, her voice clear in the quiet night, the chorus of crickets in the woods the only other sound. He leaned closer to the window, rising on his tiptoes to peer over the windowsill.

Laurie stood in the bright light of the kitchen in front of the stove, a fork in her hand, holding her cell phone to her ear.

"He went out with Jerry and his dad," she said. "They're probably just late. I think they were going to shift gear or something. Least that's what he told me. What's that noise? It sounds like you're on the boat. I would have used the radio if I'd known . . ."

She paused.

"Of course I understand, Mom. I'll have him call you as soon as he gets in. But I thought you were staying another night."

She switched the phone to the other ear. "I guess that doesn't surprise me. Can't keep Dad off the water. Okay. So I'll see you in about twenty minutes."

She paused, poking at the bacon.

"No, Jake has not been over to the house. I promise. Okay. I will. Okay, Mom. You, too."

She set the phone on the table, sighed, and blew a strand of hair out of her face. She went back to the stove and flipped the bacon.

Eddie pressed his face against the screen.

"Hey, Laurie," he whispered. "It's me."

Laurie dropped the fork and spun around, holding her hand to her chest.

"Get in here, you idiot," she said. "What is going on? First you lie to me about taking that Briggs kid back to camp, and then I've got Chief Snow calling me on the phone saying you're some kind of wanted criminal. And Mom and Dad . . . Just get inside, now."

"Should I stay here?" whispered Briggs.

"No way," said Eddie. "You're with me on this. It's time to find out if she is or not."

He glanced at the window, then back at Briggs.

"Let's go."

They ran around the side of the house to the back screen door and went through the mudroom into the kitchen.

"Sit down," said Laurie, "and tell me what's going on."

"We don't have time," said Eddie, gripping the back of a chair. "But . . . I've got to ask you something. And tell you something about Jake."

"What's all this about you stealing lobsters?" she said. She picked the fork off the floor and set it in the sink. "Sounds ridiculous to me, but Chief Snow says you're the one."

"It's Jake, Laurie," said Eddie. "He's been . . ."

"Forget Jake," she said. She rattled open a drawer and took out another fork. "What about you? What did you do?" She moved to the pan and forked out a strip of bacon onto a paper towel.

"Nothing," he said. "Nothing at all. Chief Snow spotted us when we were putting lobsters back. He figured we were stealing them."

"That man thinks everyone's a criminal," said Laurie. She looked up to glare at Eddie. "But you made the mistake of taking off. So for Chief Snow, that's an admission of guilt. Resisting arrest or some such thing, that was your biggest mistake—guilty until proven innocent. And what do you mean you were putting lobsters *back*?"

"Let me finish," said Eddie. "I've got to tell you who was . . . who was stealing the lobsters."

Laurie looked at him. "Don't tell me. Don't tell me it's Jake."

"You may not want to believe it," he said, "but Jake is the one stealing them, not us. Jake and that Marty guy, a counselor at the camp."

"My nemesis," said Briggs.

Laurie shot him a look.

"I thought something was fishy when you guys were here this morning. You should be ashamed. Do you know how many people are out hunting for you? Even Jake is, now that I told him I'd seen you."

Eddie and Briggs looked at each other.

"Laurie," said Eddie. "What did you tell him?"

"I don't know," she said, poking at the bacon. A bubble

of fat snapped and she jerked her arm back, then rubbed her forearm. "It was right around five, around my dinner break, when he swung by the way he usually does when he's not out fishing. Man that stings."

She brushed her hair off her forehead.

"I lied for you again, Eddie," she said. "Something I'm through with. I told him I saw you and that you were heading back out to Greenhead, to see how the bassing was on the turn of the tide. That maybe you'd bump into each other since he'd said something about heading out there again, too. And I didn't say a word to anyone else all day because I didn't want to ruin your big moment when you brought Briggs back to camp. Am I a sucker or what?"

"Did you tell Jake about Chief Snow, that he thinks we're the thieves?"

"No, I didn't get Chief Snow's message till I got home from work."

Eddie shook his head. "So Jake thinks we went back to Greenhead. Laurie, you have to listen to me. We didn't do it. And Jake said he'd . . . well, he said if we went back to Greenhead, he was going to make us pay. When I went fishing this morning, I found out where they were taking the lobsters. They keep them in a tidal pool on Greenhead. I heard them talking. It was them. So we took some lobsters back, and that's when Chief Snow saw us."

Laurie fished the last of the bacon out of the pan, then sat down at the kitchen table and rubbed her forearm.

"Look," said Eddie, scraping out a chair and sitting down. "You've got to believe me. Remember how empty the lobster car was? We put lobsters back in. Go take a look. It's Jake who stole them. Do you understand? I saw him. I saw Marty. I saw the lobsters. We even have . . . had . . . a picture of them stealing from Philbrick. Didn't we, Briggs?"

Laurie turned to look at Briggs.

"Yes to the latter," he said. "And I saw more lobsters in that pool than I've seen anywhere else."

"It's not that," said Laurie. "I believe you. I'm just thinking about Jake. I asked him how the bassing was going a while back, and he said great. I said that if it was going so great, why didn't he bring one over for dinner sometime? Never did. Always made an excuse. Needed the money, he said. And you know what? I thought, 'He's not really bassing, is he?'"

She looked at Eddie.

"I should have realized what was happening. No, that's not true. I knew it. I knew something was wrong. I knew I was being used somehow. I just wouldn't let myself believe it."

Eddie looked at her. "You didn't have anything to do with this, did you?"

She frowned.

"Why would I?"

"Well, you and Jake . . ."

She looked away. "I may go out with him," she said in a near whisper, "may have *gone* out with him, but I'm not going to rob my family because of him. He told me he's been bassing most of the summer. I was stupid enough to believe him. Instead he's been stealing lobsters. From islanders. From us. That would only hurt people he knows. Why would he do that?"

Eddie glanced at Briggs, then back at Laurie.

"I have no clue," he said. "But I do know we've got no time to waste here if we're going to get any more of the lobsters back."

He looked at Laurie. Her eyes seemed to be fixed on a point somewhere beyond his shoulder. The purr of crickets came in through the screens. He wished he'd never doubted her.

"What a creep he is," she said, her voice gravelly. "You know that overnight Dad made, the time he was shifting gear out to deeper water by Malabar and Thrumcap? That was the night our lobsters were stolen. I told Jake that Dad was planning that trip. He used me."

She held her head in her hands.

"God, am I sick of this place."

Eddie reached toward her, hesitated, then gave her a quick pat on the shoulder. "Laurie," he said, "we need your help."

She looked at him as if remembering he was still there.

"Do you want some bacon? I was starving when I got off work, but I just lost my appetite."

"Why, thank you very much," said Briggs, squinting across the room. "I'd love some. I'm famished."

"We don't have time," said Eddie. "Laurie, there's only one thing to do. You have to tell Chief Snow that the lobsters are on Greenhead, but that Jake and Marty are only part of the operation. That's why we're going out there. We have to figure out where they're taking the lobsters on the mainland in case Chief Snow doesn't get there in time."

Laurie got up, stripped off another piece of paper towel, and wrapped up the bacon in it. "Here," she said to Briggs. "You better take this."

She turned back to Eddie. "And just how are you going to figure out where they're taking the lobsters?"

Eddie glanced at Briggs, then looked back at Laurie.

"I'm not sure yet. We'll have to follow them. We'll get word to you where they're headed."

He thought for a moment.

"We'll wait for them back out there," he said. "And then we'll call you with the exact time they left and the direction they're heading, so Chief Snow can get a bearing on them."

Laurie shook her head, grimacing. "Do you realize what kind of trouble you're in? The police are after you. Do you know what that means? You know how Chief Snow thinks lobstermen are always up to no good. He probably half suspects Dad and the rest of them have cooked up some scam for all we know. He's a cop, and he's after you."

She shook her head again. "And I have no idea if he'll believe your story even if I do tell him. You know, I have half a mind to call Chief Snow right now and have him lock you up just to keep you safe until Mom and Dad get back."

Eddie pushed his chair back and stood up.

"Laurie, we need your help," he said again as he edged across the floor. "Throwing us in jail won't help us get the lobsters back. And we don't have time right now to explain what's going on to Chief Snow. We'll miss our chance to track down the thieves. You know what Dad says about doing things ourselves. We can handle everything. Always have. Always will."

"I've heard it a hundred times. But sometimes it doesn't make sense. Sometimes you need to ask for help."

Eddie looked her in the eye.

"That's what we're asking you for now."

She looked at him and opened her mouth as if to speak, but said nothing.

"Come on, Briggs," said Eddie.

Eddie gripped the door handle and stepped into the mudroom.

"We can't wait, Laurie," he said. "We're counting on you."

Eddie turned to go.

"Hang on a second," said Laurie.

Eddie looked back inside. Laurie got up and walked over to him.

"Take this," she said, handing him her phone. "How else are you going to get word to me where they're going?"

"But this is your new . . ."

She raised a hand. "Take it. Call me. Promise?"

"Promise."

He nodded at her. Then he turned and grabbed a pair of his sneakers from the mudroom. He hopped on one foot, then the other as he pulled them on.

He pushed through the screen door, Briggs following. The screen door clapped shut behind them.

"You ready?" said Eddie, squatting on the landing to tie his laces. "Need to hold on to my shirt so you don't run into anything?"

"I can manage," said Briggs. "Though you might want to warn me if you see any obstacles looming."

"Count on it, Briggs," said Eddie.

They thumped down the stairs and ran for the skiff.

CHAPTER EIGHTEEN

AUGUST 13, 1:13 A.M.

EDDIE WAS FOLDING the last of his share of the bacon into his mouth when he spotted Tern Island Light. He brought the skiff around on a course for Greenhead Island. They skimmed over the quiet Gut, stars swimming through clear patches of sky as the fog began to pull apart. Eddie saw the dark hump of the island ahead and idled alongshore till he found the strip of beach where he had first landed. They hauled the skiff into the undergrowth, then made their way toward the tidal pool.

"If they already came out for them," whispered Briggs, trotting beside Eddie, "what do we do then?"

"I don't know," said Eddie. "Stop here."

Eddie crouched down behind a thicket of bushes and peered through the branches at the marsh and the tidal pool beyond. He could make out only the dim forms of the ground and the water.

"I'm going to take a look," he said. "Let me know if you see anybody coming."

"They might step on me before I do," said Briggs. "But I'll keep my ears open. Be careful."

Eddie crouched, then broke into a run. He passed the thicket and ran to the pool. He switched on his flashlight. The pool was just as they'd left it.

So they haven't been out to unload again, he thought. *That means they must be heading back soon with more.* This would be their last trip before they went to the mainland, then, unless their plans had changed.

He switched off his flashlight and sprinted back to the thicket.

"They haven't been back out here," he panted. "Not yet. But I'll bet they'll be shifting everything they've got to the mainland when they do. Wait a sec. There's a boat coming in. Got to be them."

Eddie saw the beam of a searchlight sweep over the water, then fix on the tidal pool.

"Have to get closer," he said. "Follow me."

"Closer?" Before Briggs could say anything else, Eddie ran in a crouch onto the beach. Briggs took a deep breath and pushed his way out of the undergrowth.

Eddie raced along the sand, flanking the tidal pool, then flung himself down behind a tussock of grass. Briggs flew past him, tried to stop, slipped, and fell. He scrambled on all fours back beside Eddie.

Eddie listened to the engine idling, watching the

searchlight trained on the tidal pool. He saw a figure lit by the beam climb into the inflatable and start the outboard. The inflatable buzzed toward shore.

"It's Jake," he whispered.

As Jake beached the inflatable and went to the pool, Eddie knew what they had to do next.

He watched Jake haul out a crate of lobsters and stagger with it to the inflatable. He dropped it in and returned for another one.

"Looks like they're taking them," said Briggs. "Should we go back for the skiff? Do you think we should follow them?"

"We don't have time to go back," said Eddie, checking his watch. It read 1:13, and the words his father had said about not treating the watch like a toy came back to him.

What we have to do, he thought, *sure isn't playtime.*

"Ready?" he whispered.

"Ready for what?" said Briggs.

"To get on the inflatable," said Eddie.

"To get on the inflatable?" said Briggs. "Is that what you said?"

"If we don't go," said Eddie, "there's no way we'll know for sure where they're taking the lobsters."

"Shouldn't we just call Laurie now and let Jake and Marty be on their merry way—right into the hands of the police?"

"We will call Laurie. But if we want to know exactly

where they're taking them, we have to get ourselves aboard. The timing's got to be right. If Chief Snow catches Jake and Marty too soon, what about the rest of the operation? Look at them. They're heading right into a trap, and they don't even know it."

Jake set another crate into the inflatable, then stepped in and ferried the crates to the boat. Marty came to the stern.

"Step on it," Marty called. "You know what Deep Hole Channel is like at dead low."

Deep Hole, thought Eddie. *So that's where they're going*—a cove with an abandoned dock on the mainland.

"Okay," he said. "Once they're done loading, we have to cut around that way and swim to the inflatable."

"Never did I imagine," said Briggs, "that escaping from sailing camp would require my becoming a Navy SEAL."

Eddie reached into his pocket and pulled out Laurie's phone. He dialed and held the phone to his ear. On the second ring Laurie picked up.

"Eddie?"

"I only have a second," Eddie whispered. The signal was weak and static washed like breaking waves into his ear.

"We're on Greenhead," he said. "They're about to take off. We're trying to get on their boat. They're getting the whole load aboard. Heading to the mainland—they said

Deep Hole. Get word to Chief Snow. The time is"—he glanced at his watch— "one twenty-two. Looks like they'll shove off any minute."

He listened. There was only static. Had he lost her? Had she heard all the information?

He shut the phone off.

"Better leave this here," he said, "This isn't any more an underwater model than your iSponge. We'll come back for it."

"I certainly hope we have the opportunity to do so," said Briggs.

Eddie shut the phone off and nestled it into the tuft of grass.

"Let's just hope Laurie could hear me," he said. "Okay, you ready?"

"No," Briggs said, "but I'll go anyway."

Eddie picked himself up off the ground and ran toward the water, Briggs right behind him.

They bent low as they entered the water and let themselves slip forward into it. Eddie shivered as the water rose to his waist. The bottom shelved away so that soon only their heads showed as they stroked toward the boat.

"Let's get the last of 'em aboard," Eddie heard Marty say. "Brown'll be there in about an hour."

Eddie and Briggs came around the side of *Nuthin's Easy*, the hull blocking them from view. Jake pushed off and steered the inflatable for shore. The inflatable's small wake lapped over Eddie. Treading water, he put his hand against the side of the boat and felt the vibrations of the idling engine shiver through the hull.

He motioned for Briggs to follow. They felt their way forward along the slime and barnacles below the waterline of the hull till they were all the way forward, under the flare of the bow, out of sight from the stern. They gripped on to the vertical ridge of the prow to stay afloat.

"When they're done," whispered Eddie, "we'll slip back to the stern and grab on to the inflatable."

Briggs nodded.

"Back in the water again," he whispered. "Can't tread water all night."

Eddie looked into the sky to see a few stars appear. The stars vanished, then reappeared as the fog glided overhead.

Jake throttled down as he returned with the crates and eased the inflatable to the stern.

"Get ready," whispered Eddie. "Start moving back."

Dog-paddling, they eased along the waterline, back toward the stern, hidden by the slope of the hull.

"That's all of them," Eddie heard Jake say.

"Get aboard," said Marty, "and let's shove off."

Eddie and Briggs swam slowly to avoid splashing the still water. On the gentle swell, the boat settled one way, then the other. The idling engine burbled.

"Hold's full," said Marty. "Just throw the tarp over the rest."

Eddie heard footsteps on deck coming toward them,

and he motioned for Briggs to stop. He pressed against the hull. He craned his neck to look up, the hull curving above him. He saw a silhouette lean over for a moment before it pulled back.

"Thought I heard something," he heard Jake say.

"Don't get spooked now," said Marty, "not when it's time to cash in. Let's get going."

Eddie nudged Briggs's shoulder and they kept moving back toward the stern, the steep hull rising above them. Now Eddie could see the inflatable tethered off the stern. He pointed at it. Briggs nodded.

Then the engine roared and water churned out from underneath the boat. The boat's stern settled into the water and the boat surged ahead, the waves and suds of the prop wash shoving Eddie and Briggs away.

The inflatable tugged on its towline behind the boat as the boat accelerated. It would be out of reach in seconds, Eddie knew. He saw Briggs splash toward the inflatable. Briggs grabbed for the lifeline fixed around its edge, but it slipped out of his hand. He fell back into the water and spun around and caught the last loop. Briggs was yanked through the water, away from Eddie, but Eddie kicked and lunged and caught hold of one of Briggs's legs. He held on, creating his own wake, his face splitting the water as they were dragged along. Briggs latched on to the lifeline with his other hand and pulled himself to the top of the tight tube of the side. Eddie tightened his grip on Briggs's ankle. The pressure of the water pouring past him increased as if he was pushing against an avalanche of wet cement.

Briggs forced himself into the inflatable and Eddie shot his hand up to grab the lifeline. Briggs twisted around and gripped Eddie's wrist. He pulled back hard and Eddie kicked in the water and felt himself pulled upward as he tumbled into the inflatable.

They lay gasping on the floor as the inflatable bounded along behind *Nuthin's Easy*.

"Let's not . . ." panted Eddie. "Let's not try that again."

"Now my left leg . . ." said Briggs, ". . . is about six inches longer than my right."

"You did it," said Eddie, pulling his flannel shirt off. "It wasn't pretty, but you did it. Just like a Navy SEAL."

Then Eddie pulled off his T-shirt, wrung both shirts out, and tugged them back on.

"Better do the same," he said. "You'll dry out faster. Even though it feels cold right now."

"I don't think I'll ever dry out," said Briggs. "And I may never get your sweatshirt back on."

Nuthin's Easy growled along, the inflatable seesawing over the slight swell.

"Need to get under the tarp," said Eddie.

"Another tarp," groaned Briggs. "If we manage to survive, never again will I cover myself in a tarp."

Eddie spread the tarp out and Briggs covered himself with it.

"Careful," said Eddie. "Your shoes are showing again."

He lifted himself up to peer over the side. He looked across the gray water. The fog was still swirling but stars flicked past in the gaps above. He squinted. There, coming through the fog, he saw the red and green running lights of a boat.

"Make sure we're covered," he said, lying on his back and pulling the tarp over his head. "There's another boat right there. Maybe someone still hunting for you."

A searchlight raked across the side of the inflatable, and Eddie saw it flash through pinprick holes in the tarp.

CHAPTER NINETEEN
AUGUST 13, 2:24 A.M.

"YOU THERE," bellowed a voice through a megaphone. "Throttle back."

Eddie eased himself up to peer over the side. A whaler swerved up close to *Nuthin's Easy*, slashing its hull with the searchlight, then slowed to keep pace with it. One man was at the wheel. He gestured to the *Nuthin's Easy* to slow down.

Eddie pulled the tarp back over him. "That's Chief Snow," he whispered to Briggs.

Nuthin's Easy slowed, then slipped into neutral.

Briggs grasped Eddie's elbow.

"Now's our chance," he whispered. "We can tell him now—before we have to go any farther."

"No," said Eddie. "The other ones on shore will get away. You wanted to get Marty, didn't you? Job's only half done."

"Hey, Chief," Eddie heard Jake call. "What's going on? You find the missing kid yet?"

"We found his boat," Snow shouted, "out on Tern Island. Now we're looking for a skiff, too, in connection with the missing kid. It's Eddie Atwell's. You seen anyone out this way? You know the skiff, right?"

"Ah, yeah, I think I've seen it before," said Jake. "But why do you want Eddie? And why would he be out now?"

"We're looking for him because we think he's involved in the lobster thefts," said Chief Snow, "along with the other kid."

"You hear that?" whispered Briggs. "It must mean Laurie hasn't talked to him—or convinced him of our innocence."

"Shh."

"They were seen taking lobsters from his dad's lobster car tonight and they took off," said Chief Snow from the whaler. "What are you out here for?"

"Well, to tell you the truth," said Jake, "I'm getting ready to do some bassing once the tide changes. I don't want to give away any secrets but I slayed them out off Greenhead a while back. I'll tell you I have a hard time believing Eddie Atwell would do such a thing."

"He's the son of a lobsterman," said Chief Snow. "No telling what he might be up to. You keeping your nose clean these days?"

"Sure am trying," said Jake.

Chief Snow cleared his throat.

"Well, you know what Eddie's skiff looks like—seventeen-foot open boat, dark green hull, buff trim," he said. "The other kid with him is tall, long blond hair, wears glasses. We're pretty sure he's the one who went missing with the catboat."

"I couldn't miss that skiff, Chief. I'll let you know if I see it."

"You do that, Jake."

The whaler clunked into gear and raced off.

When the sound of the outboard died away, Eddie heard Jake say, "You can come out now." Eddie stiffened.

"What's happening?" whispered Briggs. "Does he see us?"

"Don't know," said Eddie. "Quiet."

"That was close," Jake said. "Frosty the Snowman almost got us this time. You hear what he said about Eddie?"

"Beautiful," said Marty. "Just like Snow to think a kid would be doing this. And he thinks Briggsy's in on it?"

"You mean the kid from camp?"

For a moment, Eddie heard only the idling engine.

Then, after a moment, he heard a laugh erupt from Marty.

"You've got to be kidding," said Marty. "That is the most hilarious thing I ever heard in my life."

"That's what Snow said."

Marty snorted.

"Cops," he said. "And next time I see that Atwell kid,

he's dead meat. I had a feeling that was him this morning. Now I know it was. Same boat Snow described. But I couldn't do anything with Kendrick looking over my shoulder. If only I'd run into him when I had the boat myself . . ."

"Eddie's nothing to worry about," said Jake. "Chief Snow is. I don't think he bought that line about bassing. Not the way Laurie did."

He is *a creep*, thought Eddie. *Laurie's right about that.*

"You kidding?" said Marty. "He bought it."

From beneath the tarp, Eddie heard footsteps on the deck, followed by the engine clicking into gear. Then the boat roared up to cruising speed. The inflatable began to buck and slap over the waves. He pushed the tarp down and saw a patch of star-speckled sky appear overhead.

"Clearing," he said, just as the inflatable began pounding and slapping so hard it bounced him off the floor. He pulled the tarp back over him.

"I don't know if I can hold on," said Briggs. "Is it going to be like this the whole way?"

"Don't know," said Eddie. "Just hang on."

The inflatable skipped off a wave and slammed down, knocking them into each other.

"Sorry about that," said Briggs.

"We must be going through the break," said Eddie. "Rough."

Eddie reached behind him to grab on to a seat. Briggs

wedged his legs against the sides. The inflatable jounced along as if it were trying to fling them overboard.

"This is worse," said Briggs, "than trying to learn to ride on the dude ranch."

"Just concentrate," said Eddie. "Concentrate on holding on."

Had Laurie called Chief Snow by now? thought Eddie. If Chief Snow didn't show up on time, they'd have to think of something else to trap the thieves.

"Have to cause a distraction," he said out loud.

"What?" said Briggs.

"When we get there," said Eddie. "That's what we have to do."

"Now, don't take offense," said Briggs, "but I gather this is all somewhat ad hoc. You're simply improvising as you go, am I right?"

"Well," said Eddie, "I guess so."

The inflatable bucked hard, slapped down on the water, then shot ahead as *Nuthin's Easy* took a steep swell.

"I hate to say this," said Briggs, "but a distraction may be only part of the solution. We may need to defend ourselves—with more than our fists."

"All I've got is my jackknife."

They fell silent as they worked to keep from being thrown around. The inflatable took one great bound that lifted them high off the floor, then slammed them down.

"One more jolt like that," said Briggs, "and I'll be swimming to Portugal again."

"Tarp's coming off," said Eddie.

The next wave was gentler, and soon the water began to smooth out. Eddie pushed the tarp down to see the sky strewn with stars.

"Maybe," said Eddie, "the only option is to get aboard and ambush them."

"Right," said Briggs. "And I can hold that jackknife of yours between my teeth."

"Listen," said Eddie. "I'm serious. We could pull ourselves up by the towline and climb aboard. If we tackled Marty first, maybe Jake wouldn't do anything."

"His threat, then," said Briggs, "was only a way of passing the time of day?"

"Look, I don't know what he'd do. But we should wait till we're there to try anything." He peered at his watch. "In about a half an hour."

"I suppose," said Briggs, "I suppose it could work, but only if . . ."

A beam of light flared on from the back deck.

"Hide!" hissed Eddie, pulling the tarp up. Through the tarp, he could see the beam switching back and forth. Then it froze on them, flooding the inflatable with light.

The racing throb of the engine slowed.

"What's going on?" whispered Briggs.

The momentum of the inflatable carried it forward so it bounced off the stern of *Nuthin's Easy*. Eddie heard the engine idling and the sound of water lapping at the hull.

Then he felt the inflatable sliding through the water.

"What . . . ?" whispered Eddie.

"Hey, there!" shouted Marty. "You, under the tarp! I can see your shoes sticking out!"

His laughter rang out in the salty air as the inflatable skimmed toward the hull.

It sounds just like a gull laughing, thought Eddie, *laughing over a dead fish it just found.*

CHAPTER TWENTY

AUGUST 13, 3:34 A.M.

EDDIE LOOKED UP. Marty and Jake stood at the stern, the deck light on behind them. Marty spun his baseball cap around backward and rubbed his hands together. A grin spread across his face, one that released a trickle of fear in Eddie's stomach.

Maybe I can swim for it, he thought. He made a quick scan of the water. He could see a sprinkling of lights along the shore. At first only the distant sweep of Fog Island Light appeared behind them, but while he was looking toward Fog Island, he saw the red and green running lights of another boat in the distance. It was too far away to help.

"Well, if it isn't the infamous lobster thieves," said Marty. "And my favorite camper and runaway, Briggsy, back for more fun with Uncle Marty."

He rested his hands on the transom and peered down at them. In the garish light, Eddie saw the false smile fade from his face.

"No telling what you might find when you come out on deck to check on things," he said. "Now, you boys can either climb aboard yourselves, or I'll gaff you and drag you up."

Eddie and Briggs looked at each other. Eddie gave a small shake of his head, then stood, reached up, and gripped the stern. As soon as he did Marty grabbed his wrists and yanked him onto the rail.

"Just what do you think you're trying to pull?" said Marty. Eddie jumped down from the rail and Marty shoved him hard. Eddie staggered and fell against a stack of traps.

Marty lunged at him and grabbed him by the shirt. He drew his fist back. Eddie saw the deck light glint in Marty's eye as his fist shot out. Eddie twisted his face away and the fist glanced off his shoulder.

"Cut it out, Marty," yelled Jake.

He's going to kill me, thought Eddie, rolling away from Marty's grip.

"What the hell do you think you're doing?" said Jake, shoving Marty. Marty went down on one knee and glared at Jake.

"You guys," said Marty, getting to his feet, "are in some serious trouble."

"Take it easy," said Jake. "You don't have to rough him up."

"Oh, yeah?" said Marty. "I should take a club and do him in like a stinking bluefish."

Eddie rubbed his arm where he had banged against the traps, then his shoulder where Marty's fist had landed. His breathing came in short bursts.

"Eddie," said Jake. "What the hell are you doing? I told you . . ."

Jake fell silent. Eddie saw him flick his eyes to Marty.

Briggs swung his leg over the transom and Marty grabbed his arms. Briggs wrenched away as he landed on the deck. He tripped on a crate, falling face-first onto the deck.

"You deaf, Marty?" said Jake. "Cool it, will you?"

"Cool it?" said Marty, turning on Jake. "You're telling me to cool it? You think Brown is going to be cool with us showing up with two kids aboard? We can't let him see them. Better put them below. And tie them up. Or better yet . . ."

Eddie took Briggs by the arm and helped him to his feet. He noticed that Briggs would not look in Marty's direction.

Marty grinned. "Sound familiar, Briggsy? Which would you prefer, getting tied up or thrown overboard? Or maybe both. What, got nothing to say to that? You, the big word boy? I missed you, Briggsy. I really missed you."

Jake shook his head as he gripped Eddie's shoulder and guided him toward the pilothouse.

"You guys don't know what you've got yourselves into," he said. "You," he said to Briggs, "you go first."

Marty went to the helm and throttled up. Inside the

pilothouse, Eddie noticed a milk-carton-sized plastic box with an antenna lying on the bulkhead—the kind of emergency device that his dad had aboard *Marie A.*

The beacon, he thought. The EPIRB. Setting that off would bring every vessel and plane from miles around.

He followed Briggs down the companionway steps. The boat gained speed, the engine's roar deepening. He took in a deep breath to steady himself.

"Turn around," said Jake to Eddie. He opened a locker and took out a length of line.

When Eddie turned, he ran his eyes along the cabin wall. Resting in a rack was a stout fishing pole, rigged with a tuna hook that was almost as big as an umbrella handle.

Hook's big enough to fit around my neck, he thought.

Jake cut the line with his knife, then lashed it around Eddie's wrists.

"Let me tell you something," whispered Jake, glancing up through the companionway. "You don't know who you're messing with. This guy Brown, Marty's pal, is not a nice guy. You guys could get hurt. Bad. And Marty's right up there with him, too. You play along until I think of something. You," he said to Briggs, "put your wrists together."

Briggs held out his wrists behind him.

"Don't worry," he said. "I'm becoming something of an expert at this."

Eddie and Briggs glanced at each other.

"You're lucky," said Jake, finishing the knot. "Lucky I never told Marty about running into you. Didn't know what he'd do. Can't trust him."

"Why, Jake?" said Eddie. "Why did you steal the lobsters? My dad says he might go out of business because of you."

"Why do you think?" said Jake. "For money. Enough money to keep my boat going, get some new gear. But then you guys had to get messed up in it—that and Marty getting greedy. We weren't even going to hit your place at first. But Marty said stealing lobsters was easier than falling off a log, so why not hit as many places as we could?"

He nodded toward the pilothouse. "And then Marty heard that Brown would take as much as we could deliver. I only wanted to take them once for some extra cash. And not from your dad, either. Marty decided to make a killing of it."

"Jake!" yelled Marty from topside. "What are you doing? We're almost there."

Jake looked at Eddie and Briggs.

"Stay put," he said.

He turned and climbed topside.

Briggs sat down on a bunk. Eddie looked at him. Briggs blinked and squinted, his face pale, his tongue darting along his lips.

"I can't believe it," said Briggs. "It's my fault. Or the fault of my storklike legs and boat shoes sticking out from the tarp. I ruined everything. And now Marty . . . did you hear what he was implying?"

"He wasn't implying," said Eddie. "He was promising. But I think I can get my hand in my pocket."

Briggs looked at him. "What for?"

"My jackknife. If Marty's going to try anything, we better be ready."

The boat cruised along as Eddie strained to bring his hands around his back so he could reach inside his pocket.

"Almost there," he said. "Go over by the companionway. See what they're doing."

He brought his leg up as he snaked his hand into his pocket. He felt the jackknife with two fingers. Its metal end slid out of his grasp. He worked his fingers after it. He felt a cramp tightening in his arm, but he took a breath and worked his fingers against the ridged handle, pressed them together, and clamped it between them. The boat bounded on a wave and he hopped on one foot to keep his balance. Holding his breath, he drew the knife upward, slowly, his fingers beginning to quaver. As it pulled free, he lost his grip, and it slipped out and clattered to the deck.

Briggs crouched by the companionway.

"They seem to be arguing about something," he said. "I think it's about what to do with us."

Eddie squatted down and felt for the knife. He located it and grasped it, spun it around, and unfolded the blade.

"This sure isn't easy," he said, twisting the knife around backward to press the blade against the rope. "I'm getting it, though."

"Do you want me to help you?" said Briggs.

"Better keep listening. Marty could jump down here any second. Almost got it."

Briggs turned back to the companionway, while Eddie sawed at the line.

"Yes, they're definitely arguing about us," said Briggs. He tilted his head as he listened. Then he turned to Eddie with widening eyes. "Marty says he sees only one way to be sure Brown doesn't back out of the deal. And that's to throw us overboard."

Eddie kept cutting.

"Jake called him a moron," said Briggs. "Said if they killed us, Snow would know who did it."

"All right," said Eddie, parting the last of the strands. "That's it. There's got to be something down here we can use as a weapon."

His hands came free and he rubbed his wrists. He moved over to Briggs and sliced through his rope.

"Keep it on loose," said Eddie, "so if one of them comes down it'll seem like we're still tied up."

"There's the fishing pole," said Briggs. "Do you think we could make it into a spear?"

"I don't know," said Eddie, bending down to look under a bunk. "I'm not sure it would hold up. But if we can't find anything else, it might be worth a try. At least we have the knife."

He straightened up and leaned closer to the companionway bulkhead.

"Marty's talking to someone on the radio," he said. "Must be Brown. Said we'll be there in a few minutes."

"I can't believe this is happening to us," said Briggs. "Look. My hands are shaking."

Eddie sat down on a bunk. "Did you see the EPIRB in the pilothouse?"

"I'm lucky I can see my feet. Besides, I wouldn't know an EPIRB from a suburb."

"An EPIRB is an Emergency Position-Indicating Radio Beacon. If it goes off, it sends out a radio signal showing where we are. If we can set it off, someone will come for us for sure. We just can't be sure Laurie heard me on the phone."

"And I'm sure Marty wouldn't mind," said Briggs, "if I walked up there and asked him if I could please set off the EPIRB."

"We have to distract them somehow."

Briggs sighed and leaned on the bulkhead.

"I see no way out," he said. "We're trapped. That's all there is to it. If Marty wants to kill us now, he'll want to kill us even more if we try something. And it would give him an excuse."

Eddie shook his head.

"I don't know," he said. "We can't just sit here waiting to be tossed overboard like chum."

The rumble of the engine enveloped them. The boat rocked and shuddered as it drove through the waves.

Eddie got up.

"Well, we have to do something," he said.

Just as he stepped toward the companionway, he heard Jake shout, *"Marty! Get back here!"*

CHAPTER TWENTY-ONE
AUGUST 13, 4:37 A.M.

EDDIE PEERED THROUGH the companionway. He saw Jake wrench Marty around in a headlock.

"*I told you,*" Jake yelled over the sound of the engine, "*you're not touching them!*"

Marty lurched backward and the two men burst through the pilothouse door and disappeared onto the back deck.

Briggs appeared beside Eddie.

"Now's our chance," said Eddie. "Wait for me here."

He bounded up the steps and rushed into the pilothouse. He grabbed the EPIRB from the bulkhead and flipped it on. Its strobe went off, flashes of quivering lightning flickering in his face. He stuffed the unit under his shirt. Then he peeked out the back window to see Jake spin and latch on to one of the stacked traps. He plucked it up and swung it around at Marty and it glanced off Marty's head. Marty's hat flew into the air and disappeared overboard as he staggered backward with his head in his hands. He hit the rail, then fell forward onto the deck. Eddie saw Jake run toward Marty with a length of line. He yanked Marty's hands behind his back and lashed his wrists together.

Eddie started to turn but something caught his eye. Out on the water behind them, he spotted the running lights of a boat, now much closer. Far behind the boat, another set of running lights appeared.

He jumped back down into the cabin and pulled out the flashing EPIRB.

"What's that?" said Briggs, shielding his eyes.

"I forgot about the strobe," said Eddie. "And I think the Coast Guard will radio right away to see if it's a false alarm or not."

Briggs looked at him. "There goes the element of surprise," he said. "What will Marty think about that?"

"You won't believe this," Eddie said. "Jake just knocked Marty out cold."

"What?"

"Better make it look like we're still tied up," said Eddie. He buried the EPIRB under a life jacket and looped the rope around his wrists. They both sat down on the bunk.

In the companionway door Jake appeared, shaking his head. He reached the steps, peered below, then jumped into the cabin.

"This whole thing"—he panted, rubbing his chin—"has gotten out of hand."

"What happened?" said Eddie. "Where's Marty?"

Jake shook his head.

"Eddie, this is bad," he said. "Bad for you. Bad for me. What am I going to say to Brown? He'll kill me. Unless he doesn't care. Why should he care if Marty and I had a fight?"

He looked at Eddie, then Briggs.

"You guys stay down here while we unload the lobsters," he said. "Maybe they won't even notice you're aboard."

Eddie and Briggs looked at each other.

"Maybe you should turn yourself in," said Eddie.

Jake peered out a porthole.

"I've got to get back to the helm," he said as if he hadn't heard Eddie. "I can see the lights of the cove already."

He faced them, his eyes narrowing.

"You have a choice after all this is over," he said. "Say nothing to anyone. Not one word. I won't lay a finger on you."

He shook his head.

"But Marty," said Jake, "I don't know what he'll do even if you promise to keep your traps shut. He'll still want to . . ."

He looked at Eddie and Briggs, then climbed back into the pilothouse.

Briggs turned to Eddie.

"Do you really think," he said, "that the EPIRB is going to work?"

"It'll work," said Eddie, tossing aside his rope. "But if the Coast Guard radios . . . and if Laurie didn't get to Chief Snow, I don't know what's going to happen. But if she got word to Chief Snow about Deep Hole, the trap will work. Deep Hole is the key."

He looked at the fishing pole in its rack. His only other weapon was his jackknife. But what good would a fishing pole do?

Out the porthole he saw that a wash of gray dawn light had appeared above the silhouette of the land. A few shore lights reflected on the water a few miles down the coast. *Must be near Deep Hole*, he thought.

"We're there," he said, glancing at Briggs.

Briggs sat at the edge of the bunk, gripping his knees. Eddie saw his mouth moving like a trout's.

"I'm not sure," said Briggs, his tongue flicking out to lick his lips, "that I can breathe. I'm not sure I can move. My whole body feels light as froth. What are we going to do now?"

The engine throttled down and the boat slowed.

"Let's just wait to see what happens," said Eddie, "and then we'll try to get Brown. But remember. No whistling."

"Eddie, I've been meaning to tell you something."

"What's that?"

"I'm beginning to wish I left you on Greenhead Island."

Eddie smiled.

"This is better than that camp of yours, isn't it?"

"Not if I end up doing the dead man's float."

Eddie looked out the porthole.

"Coming to the dock," he said. "Looks like there's a truck and a couple of cars. That must be Brown."

The engine revved as the boat swung toward the dock, then reversed as the boat backed down to tie up.

In the circle of light cast by the single dock light, Eddie saw a man on the dock catch a line and cleat it. Two other men pushed stacks of crates toward the boat.

Jake switched off the engine just as the radio crackled on.

"Fishing Vessel *Nuthin's Easy*, do you read?" came a voice over the static. "This is Chief Snow. Jake, do you read?"

"Get these bugs unloaded now," yelled a man standing close to the porthole. All Eddie could see were baggy jeans bunched over white running shoes.

"Move it," the same voice yelled.

"Brown," Eddie whispered to Briggs. He looked through the porthole to see another pair of legs—Jake's jeans and black fishing boots.

"Where's Marty?" he heard Brown say to Jake. "What took you guys so long? I've been waiting. I don't like to wait. And who's on the radio?"

Eddie grabbed the fishing pole off the rack. He checked the hook, touching his fingertip to its needle-sharp point. He hefted the pole and reel. He stripped out a few inches of line to check the drag.

This was it. He pulled in a deep breath.

"All right," he said. "I need you to go on deck and get their attention. I'm going after Brown."

"Thanks," said Briggs. "I'm the bait."

"Ready?"

Briggs looked through the companionway, then back at Eddie.

"You have to stop asking me that. Of course I'm not ready. But I'll go anyway."

Eddie looked at him.

"We'll be okay," he said. He hefted the fishing pole again. "Let's go."

They tiptoed up the steps into the pilothouse and peered out the windows. Jake was standing on the dock talking to Brown.

"I told you," he said. "It was an accident. He'll come to any minute. We had a little disagreement, that's all. It's a personal matter."

"Now what's this?" said Brown.

The sound of a boat engine grew louder.

Eddie looked out the back window to see a man on the afterdeck lowering crates down to another on the dock. Beyond them, Chief Snow's whaler entered the circle of light, steaming fast toward the dock—the boat, he realized, that he'd seen out the pilothouse window.

"Over there," he said to Briggs. "It's Chief Snow."

He glanced beyond the whaler. There was another boat coming in right behind it.

"And look," he said, his heart accelerating. "Dad's boat."

Something on the back deck caught his eye.

"Wait," he said. "Look. It's Marty. He's getting up."

Briggs pushed by him and ran through the pilothouse door.

"Marty!" he yelled, pounding down the deck. The man unloading lobsters straightened up and stared at him.

"Hey!" he said. "Who're you?"

Briggs rushed straight at Marty as he was peeling the rope off his wrists. He lowered his head and speared his shoulder directly into his stomach. Briggs and Marty flew backward and crashed to the deck, Briggs driving his weight into Marty's body. Marty squirmed on his back, flailing his arms and legs like a lobster as he gasped for breath. He rolled him over and Briggs shoved his knees into his back once, twice, three times, Marty grunting each time. Then Briggs levered Marty's arms behind him. He grabbed the line and jammed his knees into Marty's back again. Marty tried to wrench free. Briggs wound the line around his wrists and cinched the line tight.

"Get off!" wheezed Marty. "Can't breathe!"

Eddie slid open the hauling door and climbed out onto the rail. He found himself going past the pilothouse along the deck. The fishing pole scraped against the pilothouse side as he stepped onto the foredeck. He felt as if he were floating. He saw Brown standing on the dock, his feet spread apart, his hands at his sides as if he were in a shootout. His broad head was bald as a bullet. He was looking at Briggs, but then he spotted Eddie. His gray bristly eyebrows lifted.

"Now who's this kid?" said Brown, his face turning beet red. "And who's that other one? How did you screw everything up, Jake?"

Jake turned around to squint at Eddie.

"I . . . that's," he said.

The whaler slowed as it approached, then bumped into a piling. Chief Snow hefted himself over the rail and thudded onto the dock.

Coming up right behind, *Marie A.* throttled back and spun around to back toward the dock. From beyond where the truck was parked, a siren sounded.

Brown reached inside his shirt and pulled out a pistol.

Eddie felt his hands go light. A cone of shadow closed around his vision. Shivers slithered over him.

He thought he might start floating away, but he saw himself flip the bail on the reel, rear back, and cast as hard as he could.

From down on the dock, Brown raised the pistol and pointed it at Eddie. Eddie saw the black O of the muzzle zero in on him.

The steel line followed the big tuna hook out. The hook landed on the dock behind Brown and bounced.

Set the hook, thought Eddie.

He jerked the pole tip up and the hook jumped back toward Brown. Eddie tugged the pole again and the hook slotted itself around the heel of Brown's sneaker. Eddie heaved backward, and the hook yanked Brown's foot from underneath him. Brown thudded to the dock on his back, the pistol blasting into the air. Eddie strained to keep tension on the line.

"Drop your weapon!"

Eddie snapped his head around to see his mother, his father with his arm in a sling, and Laurie following Chief Snow. Chief Snow thundered down the boards, now with his pistol drawn.

"I said drop it!" yelled Chief Snow. "Now! You're under arrest!"

CHAPTER TWENTY-TWO

EDDIE LOOKED at Brown lying on the dock, Chief Snow covering him with his pistol.

"This is all a big mistake," said Brown. "We were simply . . ."

"You have the right to keep your trap shut," said Chief Snow, looking down at him, "which I strongly advise you to do."

Eddie saw Brown's men breaking for the woods. A police cruiser hurtled down the road, blocking them. They stumbled into each other.

"Don't shoot!" yelled one of them as they raised their hands.

Two other cruisers arrived and slid to a stop behind the first car.

Eddie began to feel gravity again. He noticed that light was coming into the sky and he heard a robin chirping somewhere ashore. He exhaled and realized that he hadn't been breathing.

He looked back at Briggs, who was standing with one foot on Marty's back. A policeman jumped aboard and dragged Marty to his feet.

"Eddie!" called his father, climbing onto the deck. "You okay?"

Eddie loosened his grip on the pole.

"Yeah," he said, his heart still drumming in his ears. "Now I am." He took a breath. "Sorry—that I had to call the police."

His father ran his eyes around the harbor. He looked back at Eddie and nodded.

"Would have done the same myself."

Eddie smiled.

Eddie's dad cleared his throat. "Time to get these bugs back to the people who caught them in the first place."

"How about you, Dad? How's the shoulder?"

His father grinned.

"Never better," he said.

Eddie looked down at Laurie standing on the dock, her arms folded. Chief Snow handcuffed Jake and led him by the elbow behind Brown and another policeman. Jake looked back at Laurie.

"Laurie, I . . ." he said.

"Save it," she said, lowering her eyes. She turned and walked toward the *Nuthin's Easy*, her arms still folded.

Eddie saw Chief Snow look around as he steered Jake into a cruiser. When Chief Snow spotted Eddie, he nodded and touched his mustache. Eddie nodded back, and Chief Snow turned back to Jake.

Eddie reeled in the line and climbed around the pilothouse. He set the pole inside the pilothouse door and went out on the afterdeck.

"You okay, Briggs?" he said.

Briggs laughed.

"If I could have seen clearly, I probably would have chickened out."

Eddie laughed.

He extended his hand.

"Couldn't have done it without you," said Eddie.

Briggs peered at the hand, then smiled and took it.

"But I'm glad my dad and Chief Snow showed up," said Eddie. "Jake's EPIRB must be dead except for the strobe. I doubt the Coast Guard ever got the signal."

Eddie looked at Briggs. He had found his way to the mainland after all.

"Now that you're here," said Eddie, "are you going through with it? You going to hitch back home?"

"To be honest," said Briggs, "I think you need me to protect you. And there are all these lobsters to get aboard your father's boat. After that, I suppose I have no excuse not to go back to camp—to face whatever I have to face there."

"At least you can tell Sallie Hodge how you caught the thieves and learned to sail at the same time."

Briggs squinted at him for a moment, then smiled.

"You know," he said. "I may just do that. Sallie. I *did* enjoy sailing with her. Though I won't include the fabrication about my learning to sail. I still have a long way to go before I can make that claim. But without my nemesis there, camp begins to take on an entirely different aspect. Can you imagine what my parents will say when they hear about all this?"

Eddie grinned.

"We could use your help with the lobsters," he said, "and then we'll take you back if you want."

Eddie's mother climbed aboard and marched straight for Eddie.

"You," she said, grasping him by the shoulders and locking her eyes on his. "I don't know whether to kiss you or spank you."

Then she pulled him to her and wrapped her arms around him.

"Don't you ever do anything like that again," she said, holding him out by the shoulders. "Promise?"

Eddie looked at her. He could see her eyes misting up.

"Promise me," she said.

"Okay, Mom. I promise."

"Okay, everyone," said Eddie's dad, getting to his feet. "You ready to shift a few lobsters?"

"Sounds good to me," said Eddie, turning to Briggs.

"How about you?" he said. "Ready to take care of these bugs?"

Briggs tilted his head.

"Finest kind, Eddie," he said, blinking. "Finest kind."

All ships, all ships, all ships. This is the United States Coast Guard Station Fog Island. Cancel urgent marine information broadcast. Subject vessel has been located. Repeat, cancel urgent information broadcast. Coast Guard Station Fog Island, out.

August 13, 6:17 a.m.

LOBSTER THIEVES TRAPPED

August 14, Fog Island Harbor—Three off-islanders and two Fog Island residents are in custody in connection with the recent spate of lobster thefts. Dick Brown, 54, a former Deep Hole fish dealer, is accused of conspiring to steal lobsters throughout the Cape and Islands. Jake Daggett, 19, of Fog Island, and Martin Powers, 22, also of Fog Island, are expected to be indicted as accessories. Fog Island Chief of Police Harvey Snow credits Eddie Atwell, 12, a Fog Island resident, and summer visitor Briggs Fairfield, 13, of Bedford Hills, New York, with helping authorities apprehend the alleged perpetrators. "They set the trap," said Chief Snow of the boys. "The combined forces of Fog Island and Deep Hole police did the rest." No trial date has been set.

Item in the *Fog Island Gazette*